Savor

By Monica Murphy

The Billionaire Bachelors Club Series
Savor
Torn
Crave

New Adult
Three Broken Promises
Second Chance Boyfriend
One Week Girlfriend

Savor

A BILLIONAIRE BACHELORS
CLUB NOVEL

MONICA MURPHY

Natalie,
Nice
to
Meet you!
xo Monica
Murphy

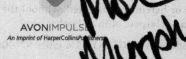

AVONIMPULSE
An Imprint of HarperCollinsPublishers

Excerpt from *Crave* copyright © 2013 by Karen Erickson.

Excerpt from *Torn* copyright © 2013 by Karen Erickson.

Excerpt from *Santa, Bring My Baby Back* copyright © 2013 by Cheryl Harper.

Excerpt from *The Christmas Cookie Chronicles: Grace* copyright © 2013 by Laurie Vanzura.

Excerpt from *Desperately Seeking Fireman* copyright © 2014 by Jennifer Bernard.

EPub Edition FEBRUARY 2014 ISBN: 9780062289384

Print Edition ISBN: 9780062289391

JV 10 9 8 7 6 5 4 3

Chapter One

Matt

"CAN YOU BECOME addicted to someone's smell?" My voice is nonchalant, my thoughts turbulent. I keep my gaze locked on the woman I'm talking about. The one I think I'm slowly becoming addicted to though my brain is screaming at me that this particular addiction is a huge mistake. Bad for me. Bad for everyone.

Ivy Emerson turns to look at me, her expression incredulous. My friend's fiancé and the mother of his future child also happens to be one of the best interior designers in all of the Napa Valley *and* she's working for me. "Who exactly are you talking about?"

Hell. I actually said that aloud? I didn't mean to.

We're sitting in my office, the door wide open, allowing me the perfect view of the outer lobby, where my assistant's desk is. Bryn James. Miss James, she of the intoxicating scent that makes my head swim and my cock hard.

Also she of the bland wardrobe and quiet ways, meaning she's not my usual type. So why the attraction? Why does her scent drive me fucking crazy?

It makes no damn sense.

"No one in particular," I lie with a shrug. Ivy has stopped by to go over the latest invoice for her services. Combine her astronomical costs with Archer Bancroft's wealth and these two will end up taking over the entire world. Or they'll just buy it all.

"You're such a liar," she mutters, shaking her head. "And you're also in denial."

"About what?" Grabbing a pen, I scribble my initials on the invoice as Ivy settles into the chair across from my desk. "Give this to Bryn and she'll cut the check for you. Do you want it now or would you like to come by and pick it up later?"

Ivy smiles. "You're also a classic avoider, aren't you? Ah, men. You're all the same."

I frown at her, wondering what she's referring to now. I've known Ivy since she was a teenager, when I became good friends with her brother Gage and her now fiancé Archer. The problem with knowing Ivy for that long is she constantly crosses professional boundaries when we work together. She has no problem telling me exactly how she feels.

Most of the time, like now, I don't want to hear it.

"Ivy." My voice lowers, and I glower at her, but she smiles at me as if she thinks I'm one big joke. The woman is completely oblivious. "When do you want your check?"

She waves a hand, the bracelets clasped around her

wrist jangling with the movement. "Just drop it in the mail. Bryn will know what to do and where to send it. She's so efficient, don't you think?"

"Extremely." I push the invoice farther across the desk, closer to where Ivy's sitting, hoping she gets the hint. I'd like her gone, so I can get back to work. Get back to possibly researching if one really could become addicted to another's scent. I've heard about pheromones before.

"She also smells amazing. I've asked her before what perfume she uses, but she won't tell me. I think she wants it to be her secret." Ivy's grinning so widely I bet her cheeks hurt.

Damn it. Why the hell did I ask her that question anyway? It just popped out of my mouth without thought, which I've been prone to doing lately when I stare at Miss James for too long.

As in, I stop thinking. My brain just shuts down. All I can do is watch and imagine what she might do if I pushed her onto her desk, grabbed hold of her long, dark hair, tugged her head back and kissed her with all the pent-up intensity that's been brewing within me since she started working for me.

Which is basically the day I first took over the winery. She came along with it. A built-in assistant, just for me. The previous owner had called her a gift.

Quite the tempting gift. One put on this earth—and right outside of my office—to make me freaking crazy with need.

All because of the way she smells.

Oh, and that sexy little voice of hers. The one she doesn't use much since she's so damn quiet. And all that hair—hair she keeps tightly bound in a bun or restrained in a sleek ponytail.

There's something going on under those bland, downright unflattering clothes too. I can tell. I'm not an idiot. She's hiding breasts and an ass that are probably pretty damn amazing.

Of course, this could all be wishful thinking since I'm still bothered by the fact that I'm attracted to my assistant—my very plain, yet very tantalizing employee.

It makes no damn sense.

"Forget I ever asked that question," I growl at Ivy, which only makes her laugh.

God, she's infuriating. I don't know how Archer can stand her sometimes.

"Don't be so cranky. It's okay to admit you have a thing for Bryn." Ivy leans forward in her chair, a secretive smile curling her lips. "I have a feeling she has a thing for you too, you know."

I do know. And I can't act on it. Bryn James works for me. She's my assistant. She's by my side constantly; we spend more time with each other than probably anyone else in our lives, especially lately what with the winery's grand reopening approaching. She's a representative of my business. If I were to fuck around with the help and the relationship fell apart, I'd be in huge trouble. She could screw me over financially every which way by suing me for sexual harassment and I'd be left with a limp dick in my hand and a ruined business.

Yeah. Not going to take the chance. Saw it happen with my father. Not going to let it happen to me.

"It doesn't matter. Nothing can happen." I send Ivy a stern look. "And this conversation can never leave this office." Glancing over her shoulder, I try to see if Bryn is at her desk but the chair is empty.

Thank Christ.

Ivy's expression goes solemn and she holds up three fingers. "This conversation stays here. Scout's honor."

"You were never a scout," I mutter, afraid she's making a promise on an untruth. She'll probably just blab to everyone. Or specifically Archer and Gage. I don't need to hear their shit.

And I am worrying way too much over this.

She laughs again. "I won't say a word, I promise. But I need to tell you something, Matt." She leans in close, her voice dropping. "She's got a major crush on you. You might not see it but it's there—sounding in her voice, shining in her eyes, every time she looks at you, talks about you. The way her body turns into yours every time the two of you are together . . . it's pretty obvious. A body language expert would have a field day with you two."

Body language expert? What the hell is Ivy talking about? "I have no idea what you're referring to, but office crushes are just that. Crushes. Harmless attractions no one ever acts on. Period. End of story."

This is what I keep telling myself. I can't pursue anything with Bryn, no matter how much I'm tempted to. Not only would it be wildly inappropriate, dating my assistant, but we come from two different worlds. She seems nice and normal, quiet and unobtrusive, and I am anything but. My life has been a circus sideshow for years.

"I get it. You're trying to do the right thing, and I admire that. So, of course you don't see anything beyond an efficient assistant in Miss James."

Well. Ivy's not too far off the mark. When I first met Bryn, she hardly said two words, kept her head bent when I spoke to her and offered lots of yes-sir and no-sir answers. She had this way of almost blending in with the walls, like she didn't want anyone to notice her.

So I didn't.

As we got comfortable working together though, something happened. I'm thinking Ivy had a hand in Bryn's slow transformation. She actually makes eye contact when she speaks to me, and she's become somewhat animated. Started to wear bolder colors as well, drawing my attention to her chest though I keep my eyes averted as best I can.

These subtle changes made me notice all of the little things—like the color of her eyes (blue), how her hair looks (like silk and I want to touch it), and the tempting fullness of her lips (they're fucking spectacular).

Her gaze lingers when she looks at me and sometimes so does mine. Her smile softens, her voice drops lower when she speaks, sparking my imagination. Would she sound like that right before I kissed her? Took off her clothes? Took her to my bed?

Yeah. All of those are dangerous thoughts. I almost prefer the old Miss James. The one who was like the wallpaper—boring and nondescript. Mean to say, but hell, the last thing I need is a distraction.

And she's become the biggest distraction I'm currently facing. The very last one I need.

"She's a great assistant. That's it. Stop trying to make something out of it that it's not," I say, sounding like an irritable old man.

"Oh, come on. You can admit you're attracted to her. You won the bet, Matt—fair and square." Her eyes sparkle. "Give in now and Gage and Archer can't give you any grief over it."

"I think you just like giving me shit," I tell her.

The million-dollar bet—like I've collected anything from either of those asshole friends of mine who owe me five hundred thousand each. When we were at a friend's wedding reception almost a year ago, they'd readily agreed to my suggestion, like fools. I'd proposed that the last single man standing would win one million bucks. It had started out as a joke. I figured Archer and Gage would be the last guys to fall in love, especially Archer. I never believed they'd take me or the bet seriously.

But surprisingly enough, they did. And I started to realize that I had them.

Archer had gone first. Gage fell right after him. They hadn't been able to hold out for even six months. Hell, Archer ran out the very night we made the bet and hooked up with Ivy.

Crazy. It's like the bet spurred them on to find a woman and fall in love.

Ivy's laughter pushes me from my thoughts, and I glance up to find her standing, snatching the invoice from my desk and clutching it in her hand. "I do like giving you shit. And I should go. It was lovely as ever to spend a few minutes in your company, Mr. DeLuca. Can't wait to see you next week when we start putting everything together for the reopening."

"See ya," I toss out, but she's already gone, escaping my office and dropping the invoice off on Bryn's desk before she disappears completely from view.

I lean back in my chair, scrub my hand across my jaw, the scruff on my face abrading my palm. I need a shave. I need a fucking vacation. I've been doing nothing but work, work, work, since I picked up this winery on a whim.

I thought it would be fun. Something different. I'd been looking for something to do after my spectacular demise from the National Baseball League.

I'd spent my formative years on a baseball field. I lived and breathed that shit and turned it into a career. I'd planned on lasting much longer than my father ever had. Planned on having a better career than he did too.

That had all come crashing down when I was running backward on the field, ready to catch a fly ball and fucking tripped. On what, I can't even remember. My own feet? No one could figure it out.

All I know is I was on top of the world, practicing for a big game, and then I was in the hospital ready to be put under for extensive knee surgery.

My career was over and I'd only played eight seasons. My entire life had changed completely, and I was at a loss as to what I should do next.

Archer kept trying to encourage both Gage and me to come to the Napa Valley. And once I was pushed into early retirement, I decided to go on the hunt for an interesting investment and possible distraction.

Within days, I found it—an established winery that had once been the pride of the area and had fallen on hard times when the patriarch died. The winery was in foreclosure. Before it went to a bankruptcy auction, I scooped it up for a song.

And found myself with a handful of employees—including one Miss Bryn James—looking at me as their personal savior.

Turned out the problem hadn't been the employees or the wine that was produced. It was the squandering of money on the part of the eldest son who'd taken over and spent lavishly on everything and nothing. He'd bled the company and his family's coffers completely dry—left it to flounder with lackluster marketing, dated labeling, and no projected plan for the next six months, let alone the next five years.

The place had been destined to fail.

So I snapped up the property, slapped my name on it and the DeLuca Winery was born. I've worked these past months nonstop, preparing for the grand reopening. The majority of the locals, especially the local vintners, think I'm a joke. That I'm the big, bad, and early retired baseball player Matthew DeLuca coming into town and playing like I know how to own a winery. Like I came here looking for a hobby and the winery is it.

They're sort of right, not that I'd ever admit it.

I want to prove them wrong. I want to show them I know exactly what the hell I'm doing. I want respect.

Unlike my father, who'd held respect in his hands time and again and then crushed it until it disintegrated into dust.

I'm nothing like him. He's a joke. The public tried to make me out to be a joke too. And they probably will again. I need to prove once and for all that just because I'm Vinnie DeLuca's son, that doesn't mean I'm just like him.

That's why I need to stay far away from Miss James. She's sweet, but she's a female who works for me. And that could cause all sorts of trouble.

Trouble I absolutely do not need.

Bryn

I SETTLE IN behind my desk, grabbing the invoice Ivy left and add it to my stack of things I need to do before I leave for the day. Lately I don't make my escape until past six, but today I have a feeling I'm going to stay even longer.

With the grand reopening happening in little over a week, there's still so much to do. Plus I guess I need to make some time to go shopping this weekend with Ivy and find a dress. Not that Matt doesn't pay me well, but I really can't afford such a splurge, especially on a dress I'll probably only wear once before I shove it into the back of my closet.

Still, I want to look my very best for Matt—as a representative of the DeLuca Winery of course.

Of course. It doesn't matter that you think he's so gorgeous your head spins every time he looks in your direc-

tion. Or when he flashes that smile. Or when you spend time in his office, just you and him, working together, his voice a low murmur, his clean masculine scent lingering in the air, driving you wild. The way he looks at you when he thinks you're not paying attention. Like maybe he wants to slowly strip your clothes off and run his hands all over your bare skin. Followed up by his mouth.

Sighing, I hang my head, staring at my keyboard before me. Having the hots for my boss is just about the stupidest thing I've ever done. And I've done plenty of stupid things in the past.

I roll my eyes and start typing. Even my thoughts go round in circles. I make no sense in my head, worrying about the going-nowhere crush on my boss. So how can I ever make sense when I'm talking to Matt? I get around him and my brain literally short circuits. He approaches my desk, and I feel a little dizzy. He smiles at me, and my heart skips about five beats.

What's worse? I've gone down this road before. And not only a crush; I let my former boss chase me around his desk a couple of times, his quick hands grabbing my ass. My breasts. I'd slapped him away but giggled. Then I'd gone and let him kiss me.

A lot.

Then I found out he had a wife and children and, oh my God, I'd wanted to die. I quit the very next day. I'd been all of nineteen, scared out of my mind and afraid his wife would come after me. And with just cause, since I kissed her husband. How could I do such a terrible thing? What was wrong with me?

You were born with that pretty body and that gorgeous face, my grandma told me long, long ago. *It will bring you nothing but trouble girl. Y'all are too pretty for words.*

I grimace, my fingers poised over the keyboard in midtap. Great. Now my grandma is haunting my thoughts. But those words she said—and what happened with my old boss—are the reason I began downplaying my looks. My face caused me so much trouble.

When I was a little girl, the known pervert who lived in the trailer three spots down tried to drag me into his car. I'd done what my mama always told me to do if someone ever tried to snatch me up—I spit in his face and ran away.

And when I was in high school and three jocks from the football team cornered me in the empty gymnasium, shoved me to my knees and were ready to take turns using my services—by sticking their dicks in my mouth—until their coach found us and told them to get lost. No one ever talked about it again.

That had been the absolute scariest moment of my life, beyond the town pervert.

So when my former sweet-talking boss worked his magic charms and somehow I found myself kissing him with all the pent-up desire of a naive, nineteen-year-old girl who's read too many romance novels, it's no surprise that my silly dreams were crushed in an instant.

My silly dreams were always crushed. And the one thing that always got me in trouble was my too-pretty face.

I moved away, left Texas and headed for California, the land of dreams and fortune. I tried my best to stick it out in Hollywood, thinking if I had the looks, I may as well try and use them.

Instead, I realized quickly I was one of a bazillion pretty faces. I nabbed one local commercial for a TV station that only aired during late night programming. I posed at a couple of car shows in a bikini and had to slap at all the men's grabby hands when they tried to rub my thigh or pinch my butt.

Dejected, I started searching online for a job. Any job, anywhere, I didn't care, I just wanted out of Hollywood. Yet again, my dreams were smashed into bits. No one wanted to give me a job unless I had sex with them. Or gave them a blow job. For some reason they all wanted blow jobs.

Perverts.

Finally I came across a help-wanted ad on Craigslist for a personal assistant in the Napa Valley. That would get me out of Hollywood but keep me in California so I wouldn't have to return home and hear how everyone thought I was an epic failure.

So I transformed myself. I got the job and started wearing no makeup, pulled my hair into a bun or ponytail and found a new wardrobe that consisted of neutral-colored, downright baggy clothing. I was a shadow of my former self. I was quiet. And I was a damn good worker.

Unfortunately, the previous owner of the winery was a terrible boss.

When he lost all his money and the property went

into foreclosure, I thought for sure I'd have to return to my dusty hometown, the place where dreams went to die. I'd started packing my bags, looking for a way to sell what little furniture I had in my crap apartment that I could barely afford when my very own personal hero came into my life and changed it forever.

Matthew DeLuca.

The sexy-as-hell former pro baseball player was forced into retirement with a career-ending knee injury. With his movie-star good looks and the easygoing smile, he walked into the building and declared in that deep, rumbly voice of his—the one that stirs my body to life every time I hear it—that he was going to change our lives for the better.

And he did.

Not only did he give us all the back pay that our former employer cheated us out of when the last few paychecks started bouncing, he gave all employees of the Chandler Winery, now under the name DeLuca, a raise and then asked if we wouldn't mind working a bit of overtime the next few months in preparation for the winery's re-opening.

He didn't have to ask any of us twice. We were more than willing to do whatever it took to make our new boss happy. And to put more money in our pockets.

Not only did Matt save my life, he was also a good boss. Fair, intelligent, generous, he pushed me hard to want to perform at the best of my ability. And he didn't try and chase me around his desk so he could steal a kiss.

Though I wish sometimes he would.

"Miss James, could you prepare an updated list of who will be attending next week's party?"

Matt's crisp, business-like tone shakes me from my thoughts, and I glance up to find him standing in front of my desk, a concerned expression etched into his features. His brow is wrinkled, his head tilted to the side, as if he's trying to figure out exactly what's wrong with me.

Certainly can't tell him that *he's* what's wrong with me, now can I?

"Yes sir." I give him a close-lipped smile, my new standard since my old one was bright and toothy and caused way too many problems. Gave men the wrong impression.

"You have plans to attend, correct?" One dark brow rises as he waits for my answer.

My mouth goes dry, I lick my lips, and notice the way his gaze falls to my mouth for the briefest moment before he looks me in the eye once more. "Correct," I say, mimicking him. I need to be there to make sure everything goes well. Even though I'm beyond intimidated to even show up.

What if . . . what if he brings a date? I'll be devastated. I'll have to pretend everything's fine and carry on with my job, but inside, I'll die a little.

Which is dumb. Dumb, dumb, dumb.

"Good." He nods once. "I need you there."

"I'll be there," I say weakly, thankful I'm sitting down since my knees feel a little wobbly. Heaven help me, I like the fact that he said he needs me there.

That he needs *me*.

"Thank you." Matt nods once and heads toward the

doorway that leads outside. "I'll be out in the orchard. Text me if you need me."

"Will do. And have fun," I call to him, my gaze dropping to his jean-clad backside. He'd dressed casually from the very start, considering he spent much of his time out in the vineyards, learning what it took to produce a quality grape that would, in turn, produce a quality wine. He wears jeans and button-down shirts that he often rolls up to the elbow, revealing those strong, tanned forearms that make my mouth water.

On occasion, he shows up in a suit. Usually when he has a meeting at the office with someone important. An investor, a wholesaler, and the like. Those days are the worst. My concentration is shot. The man can fill out a suit like no other. Those wide shoulders and broad chest, the dark hair that's a little longish in the back—a throwback to his baseball playing days, I swear. His thick, brown hair waves at the ends in the most appealing way. As in, always making my fingers itch to comb through it.

I barely restrain myself. The man is like a drug, and I'm hopelessly addicted. Not only hopelessly, I'm happily addicted. It's ridiculous, how much I think about him.

But he doesn't seem to think about me whatsoever.

My cell phone rings, and I see that it's Ivy, so I answer. I don't like taking personal calls at work. Not that Matt's ever said anything, but it doesn't feel right.

And not that I get a bunch of personal calls. I don't have a lot of friends since I'm still relatively new to the area. I don't have a boyfriend because men are nothing but trouble, and my grandma certainly never calls me. She acts like I don't even exist most of the time.

"You must come shopping with me this Saturday," she declares when I answer.

Dread sinks my stomach to my toes. I wanted to. I let her talk me into it. But the more I've thought it over, the more I've realized I can't afford the places she shops at. She's loaded. I am definitely not. "Ivy, I appreciate you wanting to take me out, but I really can't spend too much money on the dress," I explain to her turning my chair, so I can stare out the window that faces the nearby vineyards.

I can see Matt out there, talking to the field manager, his hair gleaming in the sunlight, his white button-down stretched across his shoulders in the most appealing manner. "I'm going to hit up Ross or someplace," I go on. "That's more the price range I'm looking at for this."

"You are so not going to Ross." Ivy sighs, sounding completely bent out of shape. "I have a plan and you're a part of it so you must come shopping with me. And I'm bringing a friend. You'll adore her. She's my brother's girlfriend and she's a total sweetheart."

Great. I know Ivy's brother Gage Emerson is a high-powered real estate hotshot who helped Matt find the winery in the first place. He's rich and gorgeous. Just like Matt. Just like Ivy's fiancé, Archer Bancroft.

And then there's me, little ol' Bryn James from Cactus, Texas who grew up in a doublewide and was dirt-poor my entire life. I shed my skin like the snakes that lived beneath our mobile home and started a new life. Here, in California, the Golden State.

Some of the gold's become tarnished since I got here but it's nothing a little polish can't fix.

"Sounds—"

"Like your worst nightmare?" Ivy laughs while I sit there in shock. How did she know? "I like you, Bryn. A lot. And I think you like me too."

"I do," I say automatically, sounding like a robot.

Ivy laughs harder. "You just need to . . . loosen up. You're too uptight. Do you have any friends? A boyfriend? Do you ever wear a color besides brown or tan?"

"Hey." My feelings are hurt even though all Ivy's saying is the truth. "I bought those bright tops at the Gap last month on your recommendation."

"I know. And I'm proud of you for making the effort. But you need more color, Bryn. You're so pretty—and don't deny that you are because trust me, you *so* are. Let's do your hair or take you for a makeover or something." Ivy pauses. "Please? It'll be my treat."

"No way. Uh-uh. I don't want your charity." I turn away from the window and focus on my computer screen, my vision going blurry. Usually when someone wants to do something nice for you, they always expect something in return.

At least, that's what always happens to me.

"It's not charity, I promise. I just . . . I'll explain everything to you on Saturday. We could all meet for lunch, I'll tell you everything, and then we'll shop around downtown. How does that sound?"

Like a nightmare. Like a handout. I should say no. I don't want to feel beholden to anyone. Bad enough I feel that way toward my boss. I owe him so much and he hasn't a clue.

I don't want Ivy to feel like she has to take care of me either. So embarrassing.

"Just say yes, Bryn. Come on." Ivy's tone is cajoling, and I give in because I'm a weak suck, and I can't help myself.

"Fine. I'll do it. But I have final say on everything, okay? All the shopping options and whatnot," I tell her, my voice firm.

"Yay! You won't regret this, I swear." I can literally hear the excitement in her voice. Maybe this shopping excursion means more to her than I originally thought. "Oh, and Bryn?"

"Yeah?"

"Don't tell Matt about this shopping trip okay?"

"Oookay."

Well.

That was weird.

Chapter Two

Bryn

WE MEET FOR lunch at Ivy's friend's place of business in downtown St. Helena. The Autumn Harvest Bakery and Café is super cute and super popular, if the crowds of people in line to purchase sandwiches, baked goods, and coffee drinks are any indication. The moment I walked in I wondered if we'd be able to find somewhere to sit.

Until I noticed a pregnant Ivy waving frantically from a table on the far side of the café and relief flooded me.

I wind my way through the crowded restaurant, my gaze going to the menu, which is written in chalk on a giant blackboard hanging above the counter. The soup and sandwich options sound amazing and my stomach growls in anticipation.

Yikes. Hope that doesn't happen when I meet Ivy's friend. Talk about making a tacky first impression.

"Bryn! So good to see you." Ivy hops up from the table

and envelops me in a hug like I'm her long-lost friend. I return the gesture, oddly touched by her affection since I never really get that sort of thing anymore.

I withdraw from Ivy first and smile at the woman who's now standing next to her. She's young, with long blonde hair pulled back into a loose ponytail and cool, assessing blue eyes. "This is my friend Marina Knight," Ivy says, gesturing at Marina with a wave of her hand. "She's the owner of Autumn Harvest and my future sister-in-law."

"Stop, please." Marina rolls her eyes. "Your brother hasn't made it official yet."

"Trust me, he will." Ivy laughs. "Marina, this is Bryn James. She's Matt's assistant."

"Oooh." That long, dragged out sound is telling. "I've heard lots about you." I both dread and long to know what they've said.

"Nice to meet you," I tell Marina as I shake her hand. All formal and business-like, I sound good. Calm and collected when usually this type of stressful situation tends to bring my Texan out.

It took me over a year to learn how to talk without all those twangs and y'alls but it sure doesn't take much for me to slip right back into it if I don't watch out.

"Great to meet you too," Marina says with a touch too much enthusiasm. "Ivy's told me so much about you."

Really? I'm stunned. I figured they might've gossiped about me in passing but that's it. Why in the world would Ivy talk about me to her friend? I'm so in the dark this afternoon I'm scared I won't survive it.

We all sit down and Marina goes over the menu, explaining what she thinks are the best dishes and expounding on their specials of the day. Once we've decided, she calls one of her employees over and he takes our orders—a special perk of being with the owner.

Everyone else has to stand in line and place their order at the counter.

"So Ivy said you want a makeover."

"I never said any such thing," I tell Marina, sending a surprised glance in Ivy's direction. She maintains an expression of innocence, looking downright angelic. I see her devil horns peeking through her hair though.

"Come on, Bryn. You wouldn't refuse a pregnant woman, would you?" Ivy blinks at me, the epitome of sweetness and light and my hard feelings at being pushed into something I didn't want to do melt a little.

"You're going to use that excuse as long as you can, aren't you?" Marina asks, rolling her eyes.

I know right then I'll like Marina.

"The entire pregnancy, absolutely," Ivy confirms, smiling. "Bryn, I can tell you're uncomfortable with this, but please. I'm a hormonal pregnant lady who wants nothing more than to have fun today. And having fun means finding you a gorgeous dress and going to the spa."

Just the word *spa* has dread curling in my stomach. Spa equals expensive. I should know. I've never been to one because I can't afford it.

"You're scaring her, Ivy," Marina says, her voice low. "Stop laying it on so thick. Maybe you should tell her the truth."

The truth? That sounds ominous. But there's no truth to be told, at least not yet. Ivy merely smiles at me, then changes the subject. We talk about everything and nothing while we wait for our food, Marina and Ivy chattering on while I interject when asked. Other than that, I remain silent, drinking in the cute yet hip atmosphere of the café.

Our lunches finally arrive and I dive right in, holding nothing back. I'm freaking starved and usually I eat at home, rarely going out, only because I know hardly anyone. And, since I don't cook, I eat pitiful meals that consist of Lean Cuisine microwaved meals or premade salads I pick up at the local grocery store. After I finish, they always leave me feeling empty and unsatisfied.

Kind of like my life.

Halfway through my sandwich, I realize the other women aren't eating. Glancing up from my plate, I catch both Ivy and Marina staring at me like I'm an alien who just landed on planet Earth.

I slowly chew what's in my mouth then swallow, setting the sandwich carefully on my plate. "Um, do I have something on my face?"

Marina shakes her head. "Do you never eat? Because you're acting like a starved woman."

"I don't get out much," I admit, feeling infinitely stupid.

"Give her a break and take it as a compliment. Clearly she loves your sandwiches," Ivy says, her smile kind.

"I'm not giving her a hard time. I just . . . , we don't normally see girls our age devour a sandwich like that," Marina explains.

This makes me feel even worse. I'm an absolute pig. But I eat such crappy meals, and I really don't think a soup and sandwich indulgence will do me any harm.

"Being pregnant is absolute freedom. I love eating without worry." Ivy takes a huge bite out of her sandwich for emphasis.

"You're not pregnant are you, Bryn? That's not your excuse, right?" Marina asks.

I'm horrified at her question. Pregnant? Heaven forbid. "Absolutely not," I say with conviction.

Ivy bursts out laughing, pressing a hand to her chest. "Well, thank goodness. That would've torn our plan to shreds."

Okay. I'm done with the mystery. I feel like I'm their little project, and I don't like it. "What exactly is going on here?"

"What do you mean?" Ivy asks.

"I feel like you've invited me here for lunch under false pretenses." I hate that I'm skeptical of everyone, but I can't help myself. My entire life I've always felt like someone wants something from me. It's made me throw up walls and become ultradefensive.

I have no idea what they're up to and it's making me uncomfortable.

"Just tell her Ivy," Marina mumbles, making me even more nervous.

These women in the Napa Valley are weird. And I thought Hollywood was full of strange people.

"Oh fine." Ivy blows out an irritated sigh. "I wanted this to be a surprise, but you're getting too twitchy. We want to try and pair you up with Matt."

I gape at her. Wait. What? "Are you talking about Matt—as in my boss, Matt DeLuca?"

Now it's Ivy's turn to roll her eyes. "Do you know another Matt?"

Well, I went to school with Matt Short but he's still back in Cactus, running his daddy's welding business last I heard. "But he's my boss," I stress, thinking of another boss I had. The one with the kids and the wife and the wandering hands, the one who literally chased me so fast around his desk we probably wore a path in the carpet.

"So?" Ivy waves her hand, dismissing my concerns. "I think he has the hots for you."

I refuse to let that bit of information spark hope in my chest. Forget it. "I doubt that. I'm his assistant." Who wears drab clothing and tries to be efficient but forgettable.

"So? Attraction is attraction." Ivy shrugs, taking a bite from her sandwich.

I watch her and Marina eat, the both of them completely unaffected while inside my nerves are in chaos. It's one thing to be attracted to my boss and keep my feelings secret.

It's quite another to have others notice that there might be something between us and actually want me to act on it.

"I'm not his type," I finally say, unable to come right out and say what I really feel.

I dress like this and act like this on purpose. I don't want Matt DeLuca's attention. I don't want him to notice me!

Lately though, I do. I have to fight it every day. It would be so easy, to throw on a short skirt and a revealing top, saunter into his office and lick my lips before flashing my sauciest smile. Wear my hair down and flip it over my shoulder, thrust my chest out and let him get a look at my breasts because even I can admit they're pretty nice.

But I don't do any of that. It's not worth the trouble.

"I think you're hiding beneath that exterior. I've never seen you look better than right now," Ivy says matter-of-factly.

I'm wearing a red T-shirt and a pair of jeans, and my hair is in a high ponytail. Not a lick of makeup is on my face and the jeans fit my curvier self from a year ago so they're kind of saggy. Not the most flattering thing I own.

"Gee thanks," I mutter.

"I'm being serious. The way you dress, the way you present yourself to everyone, it doesn't feel real. It's like you're doing your best to hide." Ivy contemplates me, her gaze roving over my face, and I almost want to squirm, she's making me so uncomfortable. "You have a beautiful face."

Oh, no. "Thank you," I say uncertainly.

Ivy narrows her eyes, nudges Marina with her elbow. "Like, really beautiful. You could pass for Angelina Jolie. Don't you think, Marina?"

"Please." I've been told that once or twice. Usually by some lecherous, so-called director I'm reading a script for who's hoping to get in my panties before he'll give me the part. I don't miss Hollywood at all. "I look nothing like her."

Now it's Marina's turn to scrutinize me. "Yeah, actually you kind of do look like her."

My appetite evaporates, just like that. I stare at my half-eaten sandwich, sad that I can't enjoy it any longer.

"Where are you from anyway, Bryn? I don't think you've ever told me," Ivy says.

"I came here from southern California." I shrug, being deliberately vague.

"And where did you come from before that?" Marina asks. "You have a slight accent."

Crap. I thought I'd banished that twang for good. "Fine. I grew up in Texas," I say with a sigh. "A little town I'm sure you've never heard of."

"Now I'm dying to know," Marina says.

I'd come to California to forget my past and start fresh. I want a new chance, to be a new me. Not sit over lunch and reminisce. "Cactus, Texas, population three thousand-two hundred. Right at the tippy-top of the state," I say.

Ivy grins. "You said tippy-top."

My cheeks are hot. "I guess I'm still a bit of a hick." I am such a hick. And in this town full of rich people, where everything is beautiful, and lush, and green, I'm nothing but a simple girl.

"You are not a hick. You're adorable." Ivy smiles and picks up her glass of ice water, sipping from the straw. "Let's finish lunch and go shopping before my mid-afternoon exhaustion sets in."

"We're going to Ross, right?" I ask weakly, knowing there wasn't a Ross Dress for Less anywhere near St. Helena.

"Absolutely not," Ivy says firmly, Marina nodding in agreement.

"There are a few boutiques nearby where I think we'll find something. Something amazing to knock Matt's socks off," Marina says.

"Why are you two so determined to hook me up with Matt?" I shouldn't even consider messing around with my boss. And I don't get why these two women are so willing to set their friend up with his assistant—as in me. It made no sense.

"He's lonely. I swear, in all the time I've known him, I've never seen him with a woman more than once," Ivy explains. "He's a bit of a serial dater. He needs to find a steady woman. One he can count on."

Ugh. Well that's not good. That means he's a commitment-phobe.

"He was a pro baseball player," I say, my voice dripping with sarcasm because *come on*. "You're telling me he had a hard time finding women?"

"No, certainly not. But he does have trouble finding a good one," Ivy says.

"But he's definitely the least cynical of the three," Marina adds. "Which is to your advantage, Bryn. He's not such a nonbeliever."

My head is bouncing from one to the other, like I'm watching a tennis match. I have no idea what to believe, who to believe. It all sounds like dreamy, Cinderella-type stuff.

And I'm not one who believes in the fairy tale.

"Such a nonbeliever of what?"

"Why love, of course."

Matt

"YOU, MY FRIEND, are a grumpy asshole." Gage points his beer bottle in my direction before he takes a swig, Archer chuckling and nodding in agreement.

Assholes. The both of them. Calling *me* a grumpy asshole. I have reason to be grumpy. I'm working my fingers to the bone trying to get this winery in top shape so I don't become the laughingstock of the Napa Valley. All while they're perfectly happy and content, living with their women, established in their careers. Hell, Archer's getting married soon and having a baby.

I've had to start completely over. And it sucks.

"Both of you cheated," I grumble, peeling the label off my beer bottle, shredding it to bits, and leaving a mess on the table for someone else to clean up.

And I really don't give a damn.

We're at the golf resort's lounge, having a beer after an intensely sucky game on my part. I just want to go home. Or drown my sorrows in plenty of beer.

"Hell, no we didn't cheat, you sore-ass loser. I won fair and square. It's not our fault you never have time to play golf anymore," Archer says, his look pointed as he watches me from across the table.

Wasn't that the truth? I have no time for anything anymore. It's all about the winery. Makes me worry—

and I've had this worry more than once since the moment I made the purchase—if I've done the right thing. The winery is a huge responsibility. I have a great staff helping me run it but damn.

I need a break.

Thought golfing eighteen holes with my best friends would be a great way to ease some stress. Instead, it seemed to stress me out even more. My game was bad. My focus shot. I took endless phone calls, texted more than I swung, and generally pissed everyone off—including the fourth guy we didn't even know who was paired with us to play.

Now here we sit in the nearly empty lounge—it's a Saturday afternoon, so I can only assume all the men have gone home to their wives—talking about my shitty mood.

I really hate when I'm the focus of their attention. I know my friends mean well but right now, I don't want to deal.

"You know what your problem is?" Gage asks, interrupting my thoughts.

Looks like I have no choice but to deal. "Please. Enlighten me," I drawl, preparing myself for some sort of insult. It's how we usually operate together. We're friends, we take care of each other, celebrate the ups, mourn the downs, but in the end, we always, *always* give each other shit.

We could count on each other for that.

"You need to get laid." Gage jabs his finger in my direction. "And quick."

Hell. He was close to the money, if not right on it. I can't remember the last time I got laid. I'd been detrimentally injured over a year ago during practice, for the love of God—*practice*—and that put me out of commission for months. My career, as well as my mind, was blown.

I had no time for women during that dark period of my life. Hell, I'd been a fucked-up mess, mourning the loss of my career, my life as I knew it, and I even lost a little bit of myself. My relationship with my dad became even more strained—no surprise. He'd been so proud of me for following in his footsteps and playing in the major leagues. It was his only source of pride when it came to me. Once he lost that, he lost interest.

Completely.

When I became strong enough, I went through physical therapy on my way to recovery. I was so focused on that I didn't care about women. And once I healed, I went in search of an investment, a new career, a new focus and that ended up taking all of my time, so now . . .

Here I am. Grumpy and . . . yeah, in dire need of some sexual attention.

Problem? Only one woman has snagged my attention, and I still can't figure out why. Or figure her out. Bryn is a mystery.

And I want to solve it. Solve her.

Christ. Even thinking those two benign words makes me break out in a sweat.

"You're right," I finally say, deciding to own up to it. "I haven't gotten laid in months." Too many months to mention, the number was so embarrassingly high.

"Knew it," Gage says grimly. "You need to get out more, my friend. Hit up a bar or something."

Grimacing, I shake my head. That sounds like my personal nightmare. "The bar scene is not for me. I don't have time for that sort of thing."

"You'd have a flock of women surrounding you the minute you entered," Archer says, his brows raised as he tips his head toward me. "I hear the gossip around this town. All the single women under the age of fifty are thrilled that former pro baseball superstar Matt DeLuca is living here. They want a chance with you."

"You're the most eligible bachelor in the entire area," Gage adds.

Holy shit. These two have spent way too much time with their women. "You guys sound like a bunch of gossiping hens. Are you for real? Did you really just say I'm the most eligible bachelor?" I pause. "And that all the single women under the age of *fifty* are interested? I mean what the hell?"

"Hey, there are a lot of women out there who don't care if they're older than you. They're looking for a man, doesn't matter his age," Archer says, a hint of a smile curling his lips.

That little smile makes me want to punch him. "And how do you know this?" Anger and embarrassment war within me. It's bad enough the entire community is waiting with baited breath for me to fail in the winery business. Worse, there's supposedly a line of single women desperate to get their claws in me?

I swear I'll never have any respect in this town. None. Zero.

"I hear talk. I've lived in the Napa Valley for a while now. I have a lot of connections. Ivy's gained a lot of connections in a short amount of time with her work. We're in the know and things are definitely being said about you," Archer explains.

"Marina has lived here her entire life. She's heard plenty lately. There's a lot of gossip that goes down in that little bakery of hers, especially in the morning when everyone's grabbing a coffee," Gage says. "She says the buzz is heavy about the winery, about you. Everyone's curious."

Holy hell. This just . . . sucks. I don't want to be the mockery of the Napa wine country. I'm trying to start a new life here. Become a different person. Not be known as the hotshot player son of former hotshot player—and notorious hothead—Vinnie DeLuca. Dad played for the Oakland A's years ago when I was a little kid and earned his reputation as a troublemaker from the very start.

Many in the profession expected me to follow in his footsteps. I showed talent early. I was a cocky asshole in high school because I knew I was damn good. But I wasn't a mean asshole who always tried to get in fights. That's more my father's style.

I never wanted to be like him, not like that.

Ever.

"So everyone's gossiping about me and my potential love life," I say through gritted teeth.

"Well, yeah and so are we because we're concerned, man. You're working too hard. You need to relax and live a little. You've always been a little intense when it comes to your career," Archer says.

I study Archer, see the worry filling his eyes. Yeah, we all give each other shit, but he's being serious. He's concerned for my welfare and I appreciate that.

"The minute this reopening party is done, I'm going to tone it down," I vow, feeling like I'm making some sort of solemn promise. "You're right. I can't continue to work at this pace; it'll drive me into an early grave."

"Hell yeah, it will. You gotta find balance," says the second biggest workaholic I know, Gage.

Balance. I really have no idea what it is or how to get it.

"And you gotta get laid," Archer adds with a chuckle. "We gotta find you a woman. I'm sure Ivy has some single friends."

"So does Marina. She knows everyone," Gage says.

Now they want to set me up. Great. "I can find my own woman, thank you very much."

"Really? Because you're doing a pretty piss-poor job of it at the moment." Gage laughs and Archer joins in.

"Like I have time," I mutter. Realization hits, and I decide to go in for the kill. "And hey, maybe I'm waiting because I'm in need of my payment."

"Payment?" They both echo, like it was rehearsed.

I want to knock them both upside their heads.

"Yeah, that little bet we made months ago? I'm here to collect," I say, my voice smug. "So pay up."

"We don't owe you shit," Archer mutters.

"Who's the last man standing, hmm? I want my million dollars." I could funnel it right back into the business. Hell, I'd probably give these two bastards a share of the profits from what I'd reinvest. I'm fair like that. I take care of my friends.

"There is no way I'm paying you. That was a bullshit bet," Gage protests.

"You're only saying it's bullshit because you lost." I drain my beer and set the empty bottle on the table with a loud *thunk*. "I expect payment within seven days."

"Oh, listen to you, all formal and shit. How about we make this a little more interesting." Archer leans back in his chair, a gleam in his eye.

Anticipation rolls through my brain, hums through my blood. "I'm open. What are you talking about?"

"Give us sixty days. If you're still single within that time period, we'll pay you fair and square," Archer says.

"But—" Gage starts but Archer silences him with a look.

"Sixty days? How about thirty?" I laugh. "I won't be with any woman in thirty days, especially in a relationship with one."

"Thirty? That's too short. None of us expect you to be in a relationship in thirty freaking days," Archer says. "Make it forty-five."

"Forty-five?" Gage asks. He sounds horrified. "I still think that's too short. How about ninety? That's more reasonable."

"We never said this bet was reasonable," I reply calmly. Freaking cheapskate Gage. "Forty-five days or you pay up now. It's your choice." I know I won't be in any sort of relationship in that amount of time. Give me a break.

"I want to add a stipulation." Archer grins. "No sex

either. So no relationship, no sex, no one night stands, nothing for you, Matt, for the next forty-five days. You withstand it, you'll get your million bucks ... plus another two-hundred fifty thousand to make it interesting."

"No freaking way," Gage says.

"Yes—way, jackass. We're doing it," Archer says, not even letting him argue.

"Fine. Deal," I say firmly. I've gone this long without sex, what's another forty-five days? I can handle it.

"God, you disappoint me. You're so confident. I'd think you'd at least want to get some on occasion, you know?" Gage shakes his head, but I ignore him.

"I'm agreeing to this," I say. "I'm sure you two losers need the time anyway to gather up the funds to pay me so I get it. I can be a patient guy. No problem. But in forty-five days, I want my money. No excuses, no bullshit. Six hundred and twenty-five thousand each."

"Then we have a deal," Archer says, a sly grin on his face. The asshole is up to something, I can tell.

And I don't like it.

"Whatever. Deal," Gage says much more reluctantly. The guy hates nothing more than wasting money, and I'm sure he views this payout as the ultimate waste.

"So I hear Ivy's taken your assistant out for lunch and shopping today," Archer says, his voice casual. Too casual. "What gives?"

"Really?" Curiosity fills me. I knew Ivy had taken a liking to Bryn and Bryn felt the same. But I didn't realize they'd become that close.

"Yep." Archer nods. "I heard something mentioned about a makeover."

"Marina went with them too," Gage confirms.

Shit. Now I'm really starting to sweat. Bad enough I'm attracted to Bryn despite her boring clothes and uninspired appearance. It was her damn scent. God, she smelled fucking fabulous. Sweet and fruity yet floral and with this hint of spice that I can't quite put my finger on.

"Yeah, Ivy sent me a picture as a matter of fact. Couldn't quite figure out why she'd do that since, you know, I'm not interested in any other woman but her." Archer shrugs then grabs for his phone. "Then she texted that I needed to show you."

He hands over his phone, and I look at the screen, my mouth going dry. It was a picture of Bryn in a chair at a salon, wearing a close-lipped smile, her almost-black hair cascading around her face, down past her shoulders in luxurious waves.

"Whatcha think?" Archer asks before he bursts into smug laughter.

Damn. I'm in huge trouble.

Chapter Three

Matt

I CAME INTO work early Monday morning, so I could walk the fields and inspect the vineyards alone before anyone else got there, my new absolute favorite thing to do. I'm not a sit-in-the-office kind of guy. A nine-to-five job holds absolutely no appeal. When I bought the winery, I didn't know shit about wine besides the fact that I liked some, but I definitely wasn't a connoisseur. More like an I'll-drink-some-wine-if-you-have-nothing-else type of guy.

I preferred beer.

But I've since learned there's a science to wine making. It's a formula, with a bit of luck thrown in for good measure. The grapes have to be just so. The weather has to be a certain way to insure that.

A variety of factors play into it. Some we have complete and total control over and others . . .

We're at the whim of their command, which drives those scientist brains absolutely crazy.

There's more to my spending time out in the fields this particular morning. And it all has to do with a particular woman. I'm avoiding the office because Bryn will arrive soon, and I don't want to see her. That picture Archer showed me haunted my thoughts the rest of the day. Hell, the rest of the weekend. All that hair—I could only imagine slipping my fingers through it. Wrapping those long, silky strands around my fist and giving it a tug. Pulling her in so I could kiss her. Burying my face into the soft mass and inhaling her delicious scent.

She had on a red T-shirt in the picture, that mysterious little close-lipped smile and makeup on her face. I could tell because for the first time ever, I really noticed her eyes. They were crystal blue like a perfect summer sky.

Needless to say, after thinking about Bryn a little too much, I took a shower and jerked off. This new addition to the bet with Archer and Gage is going to kill me. I couldn't even run out and find some anonymous chick and fuck her. I could lie, I guess. Keep it from them.

But I wouldn't feel right about that and besides they'd figure me out. They always do. I don't like liars. My father is a consummate one. Seeing how his lies always ended up getting him in trouble, I purposely keep myself on the straight and narrow. I'm brutally honest. Always.

Archer knows it too, that motherfucker. It was like he set that entire deal up. He knew I was interested in Bryn and he knew she would tempt me. Always one step ahead, that guy.

The field employees start to slowly trickle in, and my phone starts blowing up with emails, text messages, and phone calls. The workday has officially kicked off, so I decide to pack it in and reluctantly head for the office. I know Bryn's there; I see her car in the parking lot. As I walk through the vineyard, I go over the various scenarios that could be awaiting me within the building:

Bryn, wearing her hair down and clad in some sort of sexy skirt and button-up shirt combo with her cleavage on display.

Or Bryn, back to normal with her hair pulled into a tight bun and the baggy beige ensemble I've come to depend on.

Worse, maybe there will be a combo Bryn sitting behind her desk: hair down, beige pants and top on, those pretty eyes enhanced with cosmetics, all of it designed to drive me absolutely wild with lust. That Bryn just might do me in—every facet of her on display, making me want her.

Clearly I have too much time on my hands if I'm coming up with all of these ridiculous thoughts. I need to focus on the most important task at hand. Today's Monday and the grand reopening is Friday. There's still so much to do for this giant event it's not even funny.

And Bryn is pretty much handling everything—consulting me along the way, of course.

Hell.

I enter the building, the cool air greeting me. It's blessedly silent, and I walk down the hall toward my office, nerves eating at my gut as I roll up first one sleeve, then the other of my navy blue button-down. I'm wearing jeans and my work boots, thankful for the casual atmosphere. Every time I have to put on a monkey suit, I feel ridiculous, uncomfortable.

So not my thing.

I enter the outer office where Bryn's desk is and stop short, my eyes widening at the sight before me. It's Bryn, bent over the file cabinet that sits just behind her desk, her very fine ass waving in the air as she searches through the files.

The fact that I can actually see the shape of her ass tells me she's wearing something completely different than usual. Second clue, there's not a hint of beige or tan or khaki in sight.

The dress is black, with a delicate floral print in hints of green and turquoise. The flared skirt stops just above her knee, which means if she was bent over the cabinet much farther, I'd be looking at her panties.

Just the word *panties* makes my entire body twitch in anticipation. Those long, bare legs make my gut twist and her scent washes over me, sweet and so uniquely Bryn I'm afraid I might do something fucking crazy.

Like sneak up on her, wrap my hands around her waist and tug her close. Let her feel exactly what she does to me.

Deciding I shouldn't surprise her, I clear my throat, letting her know I've arrived. A little gasp escapes her and she stands up straight, pushing the drawer in with a loud slam as she turns—in black high-heeled shoes that fuel all sorts of instant fantasies—to face me.

"Matt! Um, Mr. DeLuca, good morning." She runs her hands down the front of her dress, her expression self-conscious, her movements agitated.

The dress fits her like a dream. I can see the shape of her full breasts, the nip in her waist, the flare of her hips. Her arms are completely exposed, slender and graceful and she lifts one, smoothing her elegant hand over her hair in a most definite nervous gesture.

Her hair just so happens to be pulled back but not like usual. It's in a loose braid, and a few wisps curl around her face, emphasizing the exotic slant of cheekbones I've never noticed before.

Good God, my assistant is smoking-ass hot.

"Morning," I say, clearing my throat, but the word comes out more like a strangled croak. "You look . . . ah . . . nice."

She darts behind her desk and lands in her chair, pulling it up close, almost like she's using her desk as some sort of protective shield. Too late, I've already seen her, and I wholeheartedly approve. "Thank you."

I don't know what else to say. All sorts of questions are running through my brain. Like, *What happened? Why did you go shopping with Ivy and Marina? What made you decide to give up beige? Is this a temporary thing or permanent, because I don't know if my heart can take it, seeing you like this every single day.*

Instead, I go for the safe and boring. It's easier. Less risky.

"Did you have a nice weekend?" I slowly approach her desk, noticing the way her fingers shake slightly when she picks up a pile of paper, straightens it and then puts it to the side.

Interesting.

"I did, thank you. How about you?" She picks up a pen and taps it against the edge of her pursed lips. Lips covered by a slick of pale peach gloss, I might add.

It was fucking great. I went and golfed with my best friends, we made a new bet that I can't touch any woman— including you—for the next forty-five days and then I saw a picture of you and your new look. I jerked off twice, not that seeing your photo with all that sexy-as-fuck hair is related—no, not at all. Then I come to work and see you like this, and all I can think about is how much I want to get my hands on you. All over you.

"It was fine," I answer, stopping just in front of her desk. She looks up at me, and my gaze drops to the elegant line of her neck, her exposed collarbone. She's wearing a delicate gold necklace with a little charm dangling from it. I can't quite tell what it is.

All I know is I want to fucking kiss her right there, where her skin is probably soft and sweet and scented. Follow the thin, tempting line of the necklace, kiss her all around her neck, her nape, her collarbone. Lick and nibble and make her moan.

"Is there anything in particular you'd like me to do for you this morning?"

Her sweet, sultry and slightly trembling voice knocks me from my thoughts and turns them even dirtier, if that's possible.

Why yes, Miss James. I'd love it if you could perch your

pretty little ass right on the edge of your desk, slowly lift your skirt and spread your legs so I can see what you're hiding under there. Maybe lick your peach glossed lips and say something subtly filthy like, "I've got something I'd like you to do, Mr. DeLuca. How about . . . me?"

I blink, hard. Twice. Trying to push the image of Bryn inviting me to fuck her from my head, but it's just no use. She's all I can see. Her hands braced behind her on the desk, her spread legs dangling, the skirt of her dress bunched around her waist. I can imagine her wearing skimpy black lace panties, panties I can see right through.

She fucking works for you! Get your mind out of the gutter.

Damn, the state board of equalization could have a field day with me. I'm a pervert of the highest degree.

"Let me make a few calls and check my emails. I'm sure there's plenty I'll need you to do today, like usual. This week is going to be a busy one," I say, my voice brusque as I turn away from her desk and head toward my office door. "You'll probably need to work late all week, just warning you."

That statement conjures up more images, ones I hurriedly push out my brain so they don't clog it all up and distract me again.

"I don't mind," she calls after me. "I have a list of things I'm going to follow up on. I'm calling the caterer right now because there are still a few unresolved items, including the final headcount for the party Friday night. I'll come see you in a bit so we can go over everything."

"Sounds good," I say as I open my office door and slam it shut behind me.

My breathing erratic like I just ran around the bases at top speed, I collapse in my chair. Exhaling loudly, I lean my head against the back of it, staring at the ceiling. Bryn's pretty face, those sexy glossed lips still forefront in my mind.

Holy hell. She looks freaking amazing. Combine all that with her heady scent, her sensible work ethic, that curvy figure, her dependability, those damn black shoes that are giving me heart palpitations, and I'm a dead man.

Forty-three days, and I can't touch a single woman, or I risk a million-dollar-plus loss. And it's not that I need the money, it's the principle of the matter. I won the initial bet fair and square. Now those two so-called friends of mine have changed it up and put me in a bind.

It's my own damn fault though. I'm the one who agreed to it in the first place.

Worse? All I can think about is touching a woman. Well, a particular one. Sitting a few feet away from me. The same woman who just so happens to work for me.

And the only person I can blame is myself.

Bryn

MATT SLAMS HIS office door with a finality that makes me jump in my chair. My heart racing, I rest my hand over my chest, feel it flutter against my palm like the furiously fast wings of a hummingbird. I hadn't expected him to walk inside at that particular moment—with my butt in the air. I was searching through the file cabinet looking for an invoice I know I paid after just receiving a past due notice in the weekend's mail.

So embarrassing, him catching me like that. *God*.

I found the paid bill. Had started ruffling around looking for something else, I can't even remember what, when I heard him clear his throat. God, he'd surprised me. I'd nearly leapt out of my skin when I turned to find him standing there, looking as gorgeous as can be. Per his usual, if I'm being truthful.

Not the way I wanted to make an impression. No, I'd planned on sitting behind my desk when I first saw him this morning. Calm, cool, and efficient, offering a bright "good morning" with an equally bright smile. Watch him stare at me in total shock.

Well, I got the shocked stare, that was for sure. But I also noticed how his gaze had been zeroed in on my backside when I was bent over before it rose quickly to meet my eyes. He didn't say anything about my change in appearance beyond the standard "you look nice."

Nice.

How boring is that? Then he went on to ask if I had a nice weekend too, like nothing had changed, nothing was different. Not that I want him to be a slobbering idiot like my creeper old boss. But I thought I'd at least thoroughly impress Matt with the dress, the hair, the makeup, and the shoes.

God, the shoes. They're pinching my toes and I don't think I've been here even an hour.

I'd expected at least a "you look pretty" comment or something. Anything really.

But it was the same old thing. Back to work. Gotta keep on it, we're so busy, and I need you to work late, Miss James, blah, blah, blah. Just like his usual self.

Instead of disappointment, I should be glad. I should be relieved and thankful he didn't leer at me and tell me how sexy I looked and could he get a hand up my skirt or anything like that. My old boss spoke to me like that all the time. He literally asked if he could feel up my "titties" one afternoon. I really hate that word. I'd worked as his receptionist for two whole weeks when he asked that particular question.

I'd been so surprised I'd politely told him, "I don't think so."

I don't think so. I'd been so naive and shocked, I'd even giggled when I said it, which probably gave him the wrong idea.

That I'd willingly let him kiss me and touch my so-called titties within two months of that first request probably gave him the wrong idea too.

Sighing, I rub my forehead, run my hand over my hair. I'd planned on wearing it down and decided at the last minute I couldn't do it. The dress, the makeup, and the shoes were bad enough. The hair, my one crowning glory as my grandma always called it, would've made it more than obvious.

My daily appearance as the drab, neutral Miss James is a complete facade. How I'm dressed at this very moment,

I'm more like my old, sexy, too-pretty-for-her-own-good Bryn self.

Shopping with Ivy and Marina had been so much fun though. Those girls ran me ragged all Saturday afternoon and into the evening. That little pregnant and supposedly exhausted Ivy was the fastest of us all, too. She pulled out so many things for me to try on, I'd been stuck in one dressing room after another, all over downtown St. Helena.

I'd broken out the credit card and bought a few new pieces of clothing for work, this dress being one of them. Then they took me to a salon, and I got my hair cut. I can't remember the last time I had it trimmed, and it felt so good to have it professionally shaped and styled, some of that heavy weight cut off since my hair is so thick.

When they offered the free makeover, I decided why not. What could it hurt? Not that I don't know how to apply makeup. I have an entire box of the stuff at home, stuffed under the sink. I haven't busted it out once since I arrived in St. Helena. I was a new person and this version of Bryn James didn't wear makeup.

The makeup artist was good and Ivy and Marina were beside themselves when it was all said and done. The new hair, the new face—they couldn't stop going on about how fabulous I looked.

Or how fabulous they thought Matt would find me.

Those words made me nervous. I wasn't doing this just to get a reaction out of Matt. I also did it for me. To bond with these two women who felt like they could be true friends. Had I ever really had friends? When I was little, yes, I had a bunch of them. I ran around with a group of kids who lived in the trailer park with me. But as I got older, filled out and got curves, the boys started paying attention to me in a different way.

And the girls didn't really like me anymore.

Shoving those unpleasant thoughts from my mind, I remember the last store we went into before going out to dinner. They'd been ready to close up shop, the employees irritated that we'd come in. Ivy had spotted a dress in the window she declared perfect for me to wear to the grand reopening and I'd reluctantly agreed.

The moment I put the magenta dress on, I knew Ivy had been right. It felt silky on my skin, with thin straps that wrapped over my shoulders and an almost completely exposed back. A deep V in the front showed off my cleavage, and the slightly fitted skirt hugged my hips and thighs stopping just above my knee. The dress was sophisticated and gorgeous and sexy. Marina and Ivy practically peed themselves they'd been so excited to see me in it when I emerged from the dressing room. I turned this way and that, smiling and laughing with them as I imagined what Matt might do when he saw me in it.

Then I slipped back into the dressing room, caught sight of the price tag and gasped in surprise.

It cost almost my entire month's paycheck.

Immediately depressed, I took the dress off, slung it back on the hanger and fled the dressing room, leaving the dress inside, mumbling to both girls that I'd changed my mind and didn't want it. Marina followed me outside in shocked disbelief, trying to convince me I needed to march right back in there and buy that dress.

I'd been too distraught to even wonder what Ivy might be doing.

Ivy joined us within moments, her expression serious and clutching a shopping bag. She thrust it toward me, her jaw set, her mouth thin.

"Don't you dare refuse this. It's my gift to you. For all the birthdays and Christmases you have coming up," Ivy said.

I'd wanted to cry as I accepted the bag but held it together. Her kindness surprised me, especially from a woman I barely knew. My own mama wouldn't look twice at me anymore since she was too busy out living her own life. I haven't seen her since I graduated high school and she'd only come for the ceremony before she left again with her boyfriend. And my grandma would rather give me crap than a present.

It was the nicest thing anyone had ever done for me before, besides Matt repaying our bounced paychecks.

Now the dress is ready to be worn, sitting in my nearly empty closet. I can't wait. I absolutely cannot wait to put it on and see what Matt does when he gets a gander of me.

Probably nothing. He'd probably say, "You look nice, Miss James," and leave it at that.

My fist curls of its own volition, and I thump it on top of my desk, making everything sitting on the surface rattle. *No.* I refuse to accept another non-reaction from

Matt. I know he's my boss. I know I shouldn't be doing anything like this. It's risky, stupid, and I could potentially lose my job or at least ruin it forever.

I still want him. The consequences be damned. I want Matthew DeLuca.

And I'm starting to think I'll do anything to make it happen.

Chapter Four

Bryn

"You work too hard."

Matt glances up, his dark gaze meeting mine. Lines of exhaustion are around his eyes, his normally lush mouth turned into a slight frown. His dark brown hair is in complete, sexy disarray and his shirtsleeves are shoved up almost past his elbows, as if he'd done it impatiently.

Which he probably had, knowing him.

For the past two days, he's been working constantly preparing for the grand reopening. Considering it's already Wednesday, and we only have two days left to prepare, I've been here right along with him helping wherever I can.

He's beautiful despite the air of tired frustration that hangs over him, and I realize in that moment that I'd love nothing more than to grab him. Slip in between his chair and the desk, settle on the edge and pull him into me by his tie. Kiss him until he forgot all about the winery and the grand reopening and the party and everything else.

Until all he could focus on was me, a more than willing woman with her tongue in his mouth and her hand in his hair, her other hand gripping his tie so he can't get away. And he wouldn't want to get away. He'd kiss me harder, grip my waist, push my skirt up and . . .

Yes. I want to kiss his troubles away. And he'd probably think I lost my mind if I even attempted it.

"I have to work hard," he says with this rueful smile that doesn't look real. No, it looks as tired as the rest of him. "Trying to make sure this all comes together properly, you know? We only have a few days left and it's crunch time."

That's his new favorite phrase—crunch time. He's been saying it since Monday, when he had a staff meeting and told everyone we needed to basically get our asses in gear and get this place in tip-top shape.

I've worked past six the last two evenings and tonight it's almost seven. I'm starving but trying to ignore my growling stomach. I'm also wishing for my drab uniform of old because hey, dressing like you don't care also means you dress comfortably.

Today I'm wearing a new black pencil skirt that makes it hard to take wide steps and a pretty, delicate white shirt that makes my boobs look huge, not that boss man has noticed. Oh, and I'm wearing the new damn shoes I've worn all week that I've somehow gotten used to—sort of.

My toes scream with joy every night when I slip the shoes off, and I might have Band-Aids on the back of my ankles, but I'm making them work. Matt's appreciative looks every time his gaze drops to my feet for even the briefest moment make all the pain worth it.

Despite parading the new wardrobe in front of him for the last three days, it's like he's hardly noticed. I know Matt's distracted, his brain completely preoccupied with this grand reopening party. It's so important to him, for the winery to be successful, for him to do something other than play baseball. I think he's afraid no one takes him seriously, and I totally get that.

But I'm dying for him to notice me. Really, really notice me. I've done just about everything I can to get him to see me, but it's like he looks right past me.

Rather frustrating.

And I want him to like me for more than my looks too. I know he appreciates the work I do for him and admires "the way I handle things so efficiently"—this is a direct quote, one he said to me only yesterday. But what about me? Bryn James, the woman? I may be just some hick from Texas at the mere age of twenty-two who's hardly lived, and I'm definitely not sophisticated like the women he probably prefers to date or screw or whatever, but damn it, I want a chance.

If I were bold and brave, I'd *demand* a chance.

I take care of the man, and he doesn't even realize it. I make sure he eats. I make sure he goes home. I handle his schedule, knowing where he needs to be or what he needs to be doing at all times. I make sure all the little details that he might've missed are handled. I'm here for him always. Always.

And he doesn't really care.

"Are you hungry?" I ask, my stomach grumbling yet again and reminding me that yes, indeed *I* certainly am.

He shrugs those impossibly broad shoulders. They look even broader when encased in starched white cotton. He's still wearing a tie though it's loosened around his neck, the first button undone, tempting me to unbutton his shirt even more and see what he's hiding beneath the fabric.

Like I don't know. I might've spent a few hours Googling Matt DeLuca. It was easy—the man has a ton of photos out there. Some of those pictures are mouthwateringly good because holy hell, the man's body is perfection. He's posed for a few magazines over the years wearing little, and I said a little prayer of thanks when I stumbled across those after I first started working for him.

I might've gone in search of those photos again last night. Staring and drooling and wondering what the heck I can do to garner this man's attention. How much more obvious do I need to be?

He'd dressed to impress today because he met with reporters from a local news station for a video interview about the winery earlier this afternoon.

Matt most definitely impressed me. I love it when he wears suits or at least a dress shirt and tie, which is not often enough in my humble opinion.

"I'm kind of hungry, I guess," he finally answers, his gaze locked on the computer screen as he taps away at the keyboard with his typical index-finger pecking. I have no idea what he's working on, but it's definitely holding his interest better than I am. "But I don't have time to eat."

"Want me to bring you something then?"

He looks at me once more, peering over the top of his monitor, his gaze narrowed, his expression skeptical. I'm sitting across from his desk, feeling a little rumpled, a lot tired and wishing I looked as perfectly sexy as he does. "You don't need to do that," he says carefully. "Maybe you should go on home, Miss James. It's late. You've put in a long day."

What, go home to an empty apartment and more Lean Cuisine? I don't think so. "I don't mind picking you up something to eat, Matt . . . er, Mr. DeLuca." I try to keep it formal between us, and he does the same, but we both slip on occasion. There's something a little fun about addressing him so properly. Makes my wicked thoughts of him all the more lurid. "I could call in an order from somewhere you like and have it here for you within thirty minutes."

"I don't know. I'm not even sure what I'd want." He rubs his hand along his jaw. I can hear the rasp of stubble against his palm, and my knees literally go weak. I would love to know what that slightly rough face would feel like against mine, or even better—how it would feel between my thighs.

Thank goodness I'm sitting down, or I swear I'd collapse because my legs are so wobbly.

"I'll take care of everything," I say, my mind scrambling as I stand. "I'll order some food and deliver it to you before I leave for the night." I start to leave the office, wondering if he prefers Italian or Chinese when he says my name in that deep, delicious voice of his.

I stop and slowly turn to find him looking at me, his expression one of pure gratitude. "Thanks a lot for taking care of me these last few days. I know I've kept you far busier than you should be."

Smiling, I try to ignore the mass of butterflies fluttering in my stomach at his words. "You're welcome. And it's my job, right? I'm just doing what I'm supposed to."

"Not necessarily a part of your formal job description, but I suppose." He smiles. "You should join me." At my confused look he explains further. "For dinner."

"Oh, I-I couldn't." I shake my head at the same exact moment my stomach decides to grumble loudly, and I rest my hand over my front, horribly embarrassed. I can feel my cheeks heat, and I'm tempted to duck and run.

But I stand my ground instead, trying to pretend it didn't happen.

Soft laughter escapes him as he quirks an eyebrow at me. "Not hungry, huh?"

"Fine. I'm starving." I roll my eyes. Are we flirting? It feels like it but . . . not. Ugh, he's so confusing. "But I'm sure you don't want to eat with me. We spend enough time together, don't you think?"

"Do you want to eat with me?" he asks, his dying laughter replaced with this foreign gleam in his eyes. "I don't mind if you don't. Come on, Bryn. Let's have dinner together at my desk. It'll be exciting." He laughs. "We can go over the caterer menu one more time. Exciting right?"

"All right," I agree, trying my best to stomp down the giddy sensation that wants to take over but it's so hard. It's bubbling to the surface ready to burst out all over

Matt. "Let me find a restaurant. What do you prefer, Italian or Chinese?"

"Italian, of course," he says, and I'm thankful.

I prefer Italian too—especially the DeLuca variety.

"DAMN, THIS IS good," Matt says as he eats another forkful of lobster ravioli. "And you said the restaurant is nearby?"

Enraptured with watching him eat, I nod silently, but realize he's not even paying attention to me, so I answer, "Yes, they're not too far from here. Little place that doesn't look like much but is packed inside."

So packed, I drew quite a few stares as I went to the register and purchased the food, waiting for the bag to be brought out. I could tell they weren't tourists. They were probably wondering who the heck I was and not like I could announce it to everyone. I stood there, smiling shyly at everyone who was blatant enough to check me out.

This city, the entire area, has a very small town feel. I understood. Whenever a stranger showed up in Cactus, everyone went crazy wondering who they were. It set the gossips buzzing for days.

That's what I've turned into. I'm the girl who sparks gossip and makes people wonder who the heck I am. Even when I was trying my best not to get any attention whatsoever, it still happened.

"What did you get?" Matt points his black plastic fork at me. His eyes are alight with interest.

We're sitting at his desk just as he said, eating quietly and occasionally making conversation. These low sounds of complete male satisfaction leave him every once in a while, setting my blood on fire, but I try to ignore them. My dinner is delicious too, something I rarely indulge in because Italian food goes straight to my hips but who cares?

Tonight—not me.

"Mushroom ravioli," I answer just before I take another bite of crusty, warm bread.

"Are you a vegetarian?" he asks.

"Please, I'm from Texas." Oh crap. That was sort of a sarcastic and shitty thing to say. I need to watch my mouth.

"Really? I had no idea." He looks at me, his gaze intense. "Tell me more."

I shrug, wishing I'd never opened this can of worms. "There's not much to tell."

"Now I doubt that, Miss James," he drawls softly. "We're sharing a meal together so at the very least you could make polite conversation."

He's not going to let this go, I can tell. "Well, you asked for my boring life story so here it is. I grew up in Cactus, Texas, a small town with one stoplight. Wait, there's another, so make it two." I tap my fingers against my lips, trying to decide what I can and can't tell him. Not the bad stuff, which there's a lot of. No-good daddy, and a too-young mama who never stuck around much or seemed to care. Gruff, but lovable grandma who gave me lots of words of wisdom but wasn't the best at showering me with affection.

This is probably why I seek out love in all the wrong places. My head is just flat-out screwed up.

"I was raised by my grandma," I finally say. "My mom was real young and not around much."

"That's . . . too bad." He looks a little uncomfortable, like he doesn't quite know how to react.

Probably shouldn't have told him that, damn it.

I make a face. "Don't feel bad. My grandma is awesome. A real sweet old lady who makes the best church cake you've ever had." Sort of. Kind of mean, actually. She's the type that sits on her front porch with a shotgun and threatens strangers who come on her property that she'll shoot their asses off if they take one step farther. No joke.

My life in Cactus is a cartoon cliché of epic proportions, I swear.

Matt frowns. "Church cake?"

"Oh, you know. A big ol' made-from-scratch chocolate sheet cake that everyone at the church social can have a piece of. With some of the best, rich chocolate frosting you've ever tasted." I sigh, missing Grandma's chocolate church cake something fierce. Grabbing at a mint the restaurant provided, I tear off the wrapper and pop it into my mouth but it's a poor substitute for chocolate cake.

"Ah, now I see it." When I look at him oddly, he smiles. "Your accent. I heard it when you were talking."

I clamp my lips shut. I start talking about home and out comes the Texan like I can't help myself. "I left Cactus when I was nineteen, and I've never been back." And I don't really miss it either. I talk to my grandma when I can, but it's not like our relationship was super close. I had no friends. And I had a wife out to hang me by my hair for messing around with her husband though she thought we'd been up to much worse. She'd found out about me pretty quickly after I found out about her, and it had been such a nightmare dealing with her.

Thank God I never slept with him. I heard he got some other poor girl who worked for him knocked up, his wife promptly left him, and he ended up marrying the mistress.

That would've been me if I'd continued with him. My life stuck married to some loser insurance salesman who can't keep his tongue in his mouth or his dick in his pants, fooling around with every dumb young girl who works for him.

A shudder moves through me at the thought.

"So how about you?" I ask, desperate to change the conversation. I push my empty plate away from me, the bread sitting in my stomach like a lead weight. Sure had been good though. "Tell me your life story."

He smiles, stabs his fork in the last lobster ravioli standing. "Raised by my father after my mother died when I was four. Always loved baseball because he was a former pro, and I wanted to follow in his footsteps. So I did, got injured, was forced into early retirement, came to Napa on my friend's recommendation and bought the winery. That's it."

Well, didn't he simplify that completely? I need to take lessons from him for the next time I get nosy questions. "You summed that up pretty well."

"I figured you Googled me anyway, so you probably already know everything." His cheeks turn ruddy, and I wonder if he's actually blushing. "I sounded like a complete ass right then."

"It's okay," I say. "I did Google you," I admit, my own cheeks heating. There'd been all the photos from his underwear ad campaign. Those had been rather . . . enlightening. "A while ago, after you took over the winery. I wanted to find out more about my new boss."

"You hadn't heard of me before, when I played baseball?"

"No, not really. I don't pay much attention to sports, and if I do, the only one I care about is football." At his raised brows, I shrug. "I am from Texas after all."

Matt

"WELL, I GUESS I can forgive you for your football love, considering you're from Texas and all," I say, smiling at her.

She returns the smile, a brilliant, toothy flash, and then it disappears as fast it came. Disappointment fills me but I ignore it.

The more I talk to Bryn, the more I like her. I'm fascinated with her being from Texas only because that's the last place I figured she'd be from, for some reason. I assumed she was a local, just like everyone else who worked for the DeLuca Winery.

The more she spoke of Texas, the thicker her accent got. It was cute, hearing her talk about grandmas and chocolate cake. She didn't drop too many other details though. Made me think there's a lot more going on behind the scenes.

I wonder if she's hiding something. I know I wish I could—my past, my entire life history is out there for all the world to read and see, thanks to Vinnie DeLuca and his escapades.

She's actually a little feisty which I didn't expect. But I've only known the other Bryn. The beige-wearing, never-looking-at-me version. This new Bryn, with the sophisticated yet sexy clothes, the gorgeous hair, and the mildly sassy attitude is a pleasant surprise.

I like that she actually ate a meal too. I've dated women before who pick at their plates or only order a piece of lettuce and a glass of water. Not only did Bryn down almost her entire meal, she also scarfed down on bread, just like I did.

Had no idea a woman with a healthy appetite was so arousing.

"Sounds like your career was cut super short, huh." She winces. "Sorry, I probably shouldn't have brought it up. I'm sure you don't like talking about it."

"It's all right. Just a fact of life, you know?" I shrug, pretending it doesn't bother me that I lost my baseball career, but it does. It hurts tremendously. "I miss it, but life goes on and brings you new challenges."

She raises a delicate brow. "And I'm sure the winery is a challenge."

"Absolutely it is—an interesting one though. Lots of hard work, but I believe it's going to reward us in the end." I said *us*, like she's an integral part of this winery, which she is to me.

I wonder if she knows exactly how much I value her. And I'm not talking about her salary or how much I'm making off this venture or anything like that. I'm referring to how much I need her help. How stuck I'd be without her.

Of course, it's not all about finances and how much money you make, right? I have enough money to last me ten lifetimes. My dad may be a loudmouthed jerk who loves to make his troubles public, but he's a rich loudmouthed jerk. I think that's what allowed him to be so crazy through the years. When you're rich, you're eccentric. When you're poor, you're flat out strange.

Either way, growing up with my father was quite the experience. He expected me to be just like him. So I tried my best to emulate him as much as I could, but I did it with my pro baseball career.

Until the unfortunate injury that took me out of the game permanently. Dad just about lost it. I swear he was ready to disown me and it hadn't even been my fault. Though it was already on shaky ground, our relationship hasn't been the same since.

Now I try my best to avoid being lumped in with my father.

"I'm sure it'll work out. I think you might have the golden touch," she says, her voice soft, her smile . . .

It's such a pretty smile. She's pretty. Beautiful. I stare at her, momentarily captivated and I shake my head, banishing my wayward thoughts.

I wonder what she meant when she said that I have the golden touch. I fucked up one career by complete accident. I'm working extra hard to make sure this one goes off without a hitch.

Now I can only hope everything sticks to the plan. We're two days out. The grand reopening kicks off Friday afternoon and runs into the late evening, with all sorts of press events, a tour of the vineyards, a wine tasting, and finally, the party starts at six. There will be food, plenty of DeLuca wine, and live entertainment.

I'm exhausted just thinking about it.

"Well, I should get back to work," I say as I point my fork at her. When I get time, I need to go back and check out the restaurant Bryn picked up our dinner from. It was the best damn meal I've had in ages.

Wonder what Bryn would say if I asked her to go with me. Like on a date.

"You're going to stay and work some more?" she asks incredulously.

I swallow and nod. "Yeah. There are a few things I need to wrap up here before I can go home."

"Do you need me to stay and help?" She blinks at me, those crystal-blue eyes sucking me right in and tempting me beyond reason.

Staying late at the office with Bryn, I can imagine all sorts of things happening. Like her spread out on my desk, her lips swollen from my kisses, her hair a sexy haphazard mess.

I need to stop thinking about Bryn in such a sexual manner. I need to get over my attraction to her. Focusing on work is far more important than figuring out how I'm going to get my hands beneath my assistant's skirt.

Yeah. I sound like a sexist jackass even in my head.

"No, you can go home. It's already well past eight. You've done more than enough." I drop my fork on my empty plate and toss my napkin on top of it.

"Oh, don't worry about that. I'll pick it all up." She grabs the to-go bag from the floor and starts gathering all of the garbage before she fills the bag with it. She picks up my empty plate, bending over slightly and offering me a delicious view straight down her shirt.

Her bra is white, lacy, and her breasts strain against the delicate fabric. My brow breaks out in a sweat at the tantalizing glimpse, and I keep my eyes trained at that spot for as long as I can before she straightens up and her breasts are out of view.

Damn, the woman is too hot for words.

"I'll toss this in the trash on my way out," she says from over her shoulder as she exits my office and heads for her desk.

I sit in my chair, immobilized as I watch her. The sway of her hips mesmerizes me. Her walk is pure seduction. That black skirt fuels my imagination, what with the way it hugs her every curve. Her ass just begs for my hands to touch it.

Get a fucking grip, man. She's your assistant. You can't go there.

Ignoring the negative thoughts running through my head, I stand and pull my wallet out of my back pocket, flipping it open. "I owe you money for dinner, Bryn."

"I can cut myself a check tomorrow if you'd like. We can write it off as a business expense, you know," she says as she rummages through her desk. "It's no big deal."

She's always thinking, my assistant. "I'd rather give you cash right now, if you don't mind." I head for her desk, as I start to pull out a couple of twenties. "You kept the receipt, right?"

I'm so intent on digging through my wallet I don't realize I'm right in front of Bryn until it's too late. I run straight into her, our bodies colliding, and I reach out, my wallet dropping from my hand to the floor as I wrap my arms around her waist to keep her from falling.

"Oh!" She grips my shirt to keep herself from slipping in those heels she's wearing, and her soft, delicious curves nestle up close. I rest my hands tentatively on her back, just above the curve of her ass as she tilts her head up, her wide-eyed gaze meeting mine. "I'm sorry," she murmurs, her tongue sneaking out and moistening her lips.

Shit, why did she have to go and do that?

"Uh, I'm the one who should apologize since I wasn't looking where I was going," I say, my brain stuttering to a halt at having her in my arms. I tighten my hold on her just the slightest bit. She feels damn good. Too good. My skin is electric, my hands itching to search her body, and I realize I should shove her away. End this conversation now before it has a chance to get completely out of hand.

"All right then. Maybe you should." Her fingers curl tighter into my shirt, fingertips brushing against my skin, and I feel her touch to the very depths of my bones, even through the fabric. My breath sticks in my throat as I stare at her, completely fascinated with the sultry expression that crosses her face. "Apologize, Mr. DeLuca."

"Sorry, Miss James," I whisper, making her smile. Damn, that smile is gorgeous. Everything about her is gorgeous. Why did I never notice her like this before? Well, I did get hung up on her scent but told myself it was nothing. That she was nothing special.

Was I such a shallow bastard that form-fitting clothes and makeup was what it took to really make me notice her?

But there's more to this woman. She's smart and always there when I need her, which is often. I try my best to be fair and not always take, take, take, but I've been pretty damn selfish since I took over the winery. I've been living and breathing this place for weeks and months.

Bryn has stood by my side the entire time. Always there with what I need, guiding me when I'm lost. She keeps me on task.

And I'm a lust-addled idiot because all I can think about is how much I want to kiss her. Taste her. Strip off her clothing and see her naked for the first time.

My head is descending like I have no control over it, and she's tilting her head back as if in waiting, the smile fading, her lips parting. Warning bells clang in my brain. What am I doing? I think I'm going to kiss her.

Yep, I'm definitely going to kiss her and find out what those delicious lips finally taste like. And when I finish kissing her, I'm going to press my face into her hair and breathe deep her addictive scent. Inhale it until it fills my lungs and makes my head spin. I can smell her now, her fragrance wrapping all around me, drugging me, and I close my eyes just as my mouth settles on hers.

The kiss is soft. Light. Simple. I'm testing her, testing myself. She doesn't run, doesn't so much as jerk in my hold. No, it's worse. She should pull away from me and slap my face. Or at the very least, stomp on my foot, tell me I'm a bastard and that she quits. I'd let her go because it's the right thing to do.

Pulling her into my arms and kissing her is the absolute wrong thing to do.

Instead, she sighs against my lips. The softest, sexiest little sound I think I've ever heard in my life and then her hands are smoothing up my chest, curving around my shoulders as she steps closer, clinging to me as if for dear life.

That's it. The sign I've been looking for despite the flash warning repeating in my head:

Step away, step away, step the fuck away, asshole.

I ignore it. I can't resist her. I don't *want* to resist her. All those soft, delicious curves press against me, her breasts to my chest, her legs tangling with mine. She's taller with those fuck-me heels on and I'm tempted to slide my hands down, curve them around her ass and see what she might do.

With the way she's responding to my mouth on hers, I have a feeling she'd like it.

The kiss is still simple, the both of us seem to be waiting for the other to make the first move. I revel in the simplicity for a minute, wanting to etch this moment into my mind, so I don't ever forget it. The way she feels in my arms. The little sounds she makes in the back of her throat, a combination of sighs and whimpers that are beyond arousing. She tastes like mint, sweet and fresh, and I slant my head, parting my lips, ready to take it deeper.

But unbelievably, she beats me to the punch, opening to me as her tongue darts out for a tentative lick against mine—a wicked little flick that sends my body into overdrive, my cock straining against my trousers. Fuck, I want her. I could drown in her.

I'm done for.

Chapter Five

Bryn

OH GOD, HE'S kissing me. Really kissing me, our tongues doing a delicate dance that gets deeper, wetter, hotter with every second that passes. I clutch at him, slide my hands from his shoulders to circle around his neck, one hand in the thick, soft hair at his nape, holding him to me.

His muscular arms tighten around my waist, like steel bands holding me close and my skin tingles at the possessive way he touches me, kisses me. This is exactly what I've been wanting for months, since I first started working with Matt. When he walked into my life and pretty much saved it, so I didn't have to pack my bags and return to Cactus, totally ashamed and a complete failure, just like everyone thought I would be.

I've fought this dizzying attraction for Matt for what feels like forever, especially this last week, and I think he has too. Over dinner, the connection only seemed to grow, like a tangible presence.

Why else would he so readily kiss me? I know it was an accident, us running into each other, but it feels so natural, being in his arms. He couldn't deny he was attracted to me any longer and now, alone in the dark, hushed, quality of the office, with no one else close by, we can finally give in to our attraction and take it a step further.

"Bryn." His voice is agonized, sending shivers down my spine when he whispers against my lips. "We shouldn't do this," he says, breaking our kiss completely.

I stroke the back of his head, still lost in the lingering sensation of his mouth moving over mine. God, the man can kiss. I'm thankful he's got a hold of me, or I'd probably melt onto the floor. What did he say again? "Wait . . . what?"

"We shouldn't do this," he repeats, pressing his lips to the spot where my pulse throbs wildly at my neck before he withdraws the slightest bit, putting distance between us.

Staring up at him, I realize he's dead serious. His expression is somber, his eyes almost . . . pained. He's putting a stop to this.

And making me feel like a humiliated fool.

"Fine." I take a deep breath and drop my hands from where I gripped his neck. "You're right. We should definitely not do this."

I sound like every silly romance I love to read when I'm not working like a dog. And I'm so pitiful it's embarrassing.

"I'm—sorry, Bryn. I got carried away." He lets go of me, and I step backward, feeling bereft without being in his embrace.

"I'm sorry too." I smooth my hand over my hair, then jerk my top back into place, running my hands over my skirt. My hands are shaking, and I release another shuddery exhale, desperate to get myself back together and quick.

No way do I want him to see how much he affects me, especially after he so soundly rejected me.

He bends down and snatches his wallet from the floor, flipping it back open and peeling out two twenty-dollar bills from within. "Is this enough?"

"For what?" My mind races. What is he giving me money for? He better not be paying me off because of the stupid kiss. And if he thinks my lips are only worth forty dollars, then I'm completely insulted.

"For the dinner you paid for," he says, his voice gentle as he holds the twenties out toward me. "Is it enough?"

"It's fine," I snap, snatching the money from his fingers and clutching it tight in my fist. I feel so incredibly stupid I don't know what else to say.

So I say nothing at all. Just turn my back on him, grab my purse from where I left it on the corner of my desk and flee the building, never once looking over my shoulder. I don't even notice the tears streaming down my cheeks until I'm in my car, sitting in the driver's seat and desperately trying to stab my key in the ignition yet somehow missing every single time.

I burst out crying in earnest, my vision blurring, and

finally get the key in. I turn it, the engine starting with its usual dependable, gentle roar. I press my forehead against the steering wheel and let the tears fall silently. No sobbing, no cursing, no shaking my fist at myself or the man who kissed me so sweetly, so passionately, I don't know if I'll ever experience another kiss like it again.

Bright headlights shine on me every time a vehicle passes, and I wince, lifting my head. I swipe at the tears dampening my cheeks, blowing out a frustrated breath. I need to get out of here. Sitting around crying and feeling sorry for myself is not the way to handle this. I've always been a pull-myself-up-by-the-bootstraps kind of girl. It's the Texan in me; the tough take-no-prisoners attitude my grandma's instilled in me ever since I was a little girl.

A pervert chases after me and tries to abduct me? No problem, spit in his eye. My old boss tries to get in my pants? No worries, just quit. A variety of Hollywood jerks proposition me for a blowjob?

Yeah. Just walk. Find another job. Find another boss, another man with too much power who knows how to quietly devastate me with just a look. A touch. A kiss.

Throwing my car into reverse, I back out of the parking lot and drive out of there so fast, my tires spin, spitting up gravel. Determination steels my spine, fuels my anger. I refuse to let someone make me feel weak all because I'm a woman. I keep doing that. It's been a pattern my entire life. I change my look to stop men from seeing a pretty face, then let myself be convinced it would be smart to go back to my usual ways and of course, I get in trouble. But forget it.

No man has ever held me down.

Ever.

"OH MY GOD, what happened to you?"

I glance up from the letter I'm typing to find Ivy standing in front of my desk, her expression one of pure disappointment mixed with horror. Straightening my shoulders, I smile at her, going for subdued.

"Whatever do you mean?" I ask calmly. It's only been a few days since I last saw her. I know she's going to give me an earful.

She waves a hand at me, her gaze drinking me in as her nose wrinkles. "The tan-colored everything—it's back. And your hair is in a bun, and you're not wearing any makeup. Why? What happened? I thought you bought yourself a new wardrobe. In fact, I know you did—I was with you."

It's pointless to try and make a man fall for me who so very clearly doesn't want to. Despite the devastating kiss, the intimate conversation and his hot eyes drinking me in every chance he could get, I needed to go back to my original look. I wear the color beige like a suit of armor. Protecting my heart from failure.

"I did. I wore my new clothes, tried my best to impress Matt and it backfired. It was an utter failure." Reaching beneath my desk, I pull out the bag that contains the gorgeous dress Ivy so generously bought me to wear for tomorrow. "I'm returning this to you. I appreciate the gesture but I won't be needing it after all."

Ivy takes the bag as if in a daze, opening it to peek inside before she turns a determined glare on me. "Oh no, you don't. Don't you dare return this to me because you think I spent too much money on it. This is my gift to you."

"No offense, but I don't want it." I sniff delicately, hoping she'll forgive me but God, I'm still just so angry at Matthew-the-jerkwad DeLuca. "There's no point in wearing it, so I'm giving it back to you. Hopefully you can still return it to the store."

"What? Why is there no point in wearing it? What happened?" Ivy gapes at me.

I flick my head in the direction of Matt's closed office door. He's kept it closed all day, hardly talking to me beyond the occasional request, said in a painfully polite voice. I'm just as bad, replying with a crisp "yes, sir" every time he asks me to do something for him, earning an irritated look in return.

"What did he do?" Ivy's voice drops to a whisper.

Shaking my head, I roll my eyes and it sort of hurts. Probably has something to do with my hair scraped into a bun so tight I swear it's pulling on my entire face. Who needs a facelift when you give yourself a hairdo like this? "I can't talk about it here. Not now."

"I refuse to accept this." Ivy deposits the bag on top of my desk, her expression practically daring me to deny her. "You're wearing it tomorrow night whether you like it or not."

"It's not that I don't like it, you know." I take the bag and throw it back under the desk, knowing I just totally wrinkled the dress. I'm going to have to iron the crap out of that thing tonight if I'm really going to wear it tomorrow. "The whole reason for you buying it was to impress a certain someone who, trust me, won't be impressed whatsoever."

"You're talking in circles and I can't stand it." Ivy starts for the door, waving her hand. "Come with me."

I follow her outside, the sun bright and warm on my chilled skin as she leads me behind the building. She turns to face me, and I cross my arms, feeling defensive. The last thing I want to do is argue with my new friend, but I also really don't want to admit to her what happened between Matt and me last night.

It's embarrassing.

"Give me all the details. Tell me what that stupid Matt did to you to make you revert to your old ways." A shudder passes over Ivy. "I hate the beige, I hope you know."

I do too, but I don't admit it. Better to act like this is more my style and hide behind it than reveal that I actually can look . . . pretty without the beige. I wear it like armor, fighting against all my vulnerabilities. "It's embarrassing."

"It'll only be between me and you. Oh, and Marina. She'll want to know what's going on," Ivy says.

"You can't tell Archer. And Marina can't tell Gage. This is our little secret," I say, pointing my finger at her.

"I'll keep my lips shut. Scout's honor." She holds up three fingers, then starts giggling, which makes me even more nervous.

"I can't take you seriously if you're laughing," I tell

her, exasperated as hell. If Matt finds out I'm outside talking to Ivy, he might get mad. He's a ball of nerves today what with everything finally happening tomorrow. Tense and stressed and the bad, weird vibes going on between us aren't helping matters any.

"I'm not laughing about this. I told Matt the same thing, scout's honor, when he was telling me something last week." She frowns, tilts her head. "I can't believe it's only been a week since Matt and I had that conversation. A lot has happened since then."

"What conversation? What did he tell you?" I'm totally testing her. If she tells me what he said there is no way I'm confessing to her what happened last night.

"Ah, ah, ah. I'm not falling for that." She smiles. Dang, she's good. "So spill."

I explain everything. How Matt seemed interested since I ditched the beige. That I stayed last night and brought him dinner, which we ate together. How I was about to leave when we ran into each other and the next thing I knew, we were kissing.

And it was amazing.

"Then it was over. He said we shouldn't be doing this, gave me forty bucks and sent me on my way," I finished miserably.

"Wait a minute, he gave you forty bucks? What for?" Ivy practically screeches.

"Shhh." I shake my head, wanting to laugh but not really finding the situation that funny. Maybe I will someday but not at the moment. "It was for dinner since I paid for it."

"Oh, thank God," she mumbles and this time I do laugh. I can't help it. "I thought he was trying to pay for your services or whatever." The entire story is just absurd.

"I thought the same thing!"

Then we're both laughing, leaning against the building as if we need it to hold us upright.

"So I'm guessing now he's ignoring you?" Ivy asks once she's composed herself.

I nod, my laughter dying. "I didn't help matters when I left last night. I didn't say a word to him, just turned and fled like my feet were on fire."

"And then you show up this morning in your beige ensemble and it's back to normal." Ivy sighs. "What a mess."

"I don't know what else to do. His rejection, it . . . hurt," I confess, pressing my lips together to prevent myself from saying anything else. She's my friend but we're not that close. I don't want her to think I'm a total idiot by divulging my past. I've had a lot of crazy stuff happen to me. Beyond the perverts and the crazy bosses and the Hollywood creeps looking for blowjobs, I had boyfriends who weren't that great either. Men look at a pretty face and decent body and think I'm easy.

I change the way I dress and Matt kisses me. Then he pushes me away. And I wanted him to notice me. Deep down inside, I want to be more to Matt than just his assistant.

I'm stupid to be upset because I brought this on myself, but I can't help myself. When it comes to men, I flat out don't think rationally.

I don't want Ivy to think I'm crazy. Even though I sort of am.

"You need to be defiant in the face of rejection, my friend. And he didn't reject you because he doesn't want you. He's probably trying to do the right thing," Ivy points out.

Hmm. She might be right. Matt seems like a pretty stand-up guy from what I've witnessed. I know he'd never set out to purposely toy with me or anything. "It won't work," I tell her, my voice firm. "He's my boss, I'm his employee. I don't know why I let you two convince me something like this *could* work."

"No, no. Don't you dare give up. I won't let you." Ivy grabs hold of my upper arms and gives me a little shake before releasing her hold. "You're going to wear one of your new outfits tomorrow. No neutrals allowed, okay? Matt needs you on your best behavior and that means you looking your best too. There's a lot at stake tomorrow."

She's so right. Tomorrow is by far the most important day of his newfound career. "Fine, okay. I'll wear my other new dress. Not even a fleck of tan in sight."

"Good." Ivy smiles. "And then tomorrow night, you're going to the party, and you'll be wearing this dress. You'll greet everyone, be an impressive representative of DeLuca Winery even if it kills you. You will make Matt so proud he'll know without a doubt what a valuable employee he has in you. If he happens to also see you as a beautiful woman, then so be it."

Where is she going with this? "And?"

"And if he makes a move, fabulous. But I'm going to

warn you." Ivy's expression turns scarily solemn. "If he doesn't make a move, don't be surprised. He tries his hardest to do the right thing, especially because of his father."

"What do you mean, because of his father? What's wrong with him?"

Ivy makes a face. "Vinnie DeLuca has a total slime-ball reputation and embarrasses Matt constantly. They pretty much don't talk anymore."

"Slime-ball reputation? Like how?" Curiosity fills me.

"Womanizer. Liked to start fights, especially when he was playing pro baseball. There were rumors he took steroids and that he gambled and cheated a lot." Ivy shakes her head. "Matt's always tried his hardest to distance himself from his father and his horrible reputation. He's always been a pretty straight arrow."

And here I come along, going from boring and bland to obvious and desperate at warp speed. No wonder he kissed me and then rejected me. He's most definitely trying to do the right thing.

While I've been trying to do the wrong thing.

"I feel like a jerk," I say with a sigh.

"You shouldn't. We encouraged you." Ivy sighs as well. "I feel like a jerk too."

"I'll wear the dress. But I won't try and flaunt myself in front of Matt or anything. It's wrong. He doesn't need that sort of trouble or guilt." I kick at a rock, feeling crappy for doing the right thing.

"You amaze me, you know that? Matt's lucky to have you by his side."

"I really hope he feels that way," I say, my heart twisting in my chest.

Matt

MATT'S LUCKY TO have you by his side.

I really hope he feels that way.

I didn't mean to eavesdrop on Bryn and Ivy's conversation, but I came upon it by accident. And when I realized they were talking about me—and specifically my dad—I had to stick around and hear what they said.

I hated hearing what Ivy said about Dad but there's no denying that she spoke the truth. He is a slime ball and has a terrible reputation, one I try to distance myself from as much as possible.

That's why I had to push Bryn away last night. I couldn't take that amazing kiss we shared any further no matter how badly I wanted to. And damn, I really wanted to.

Listening to Bryn say she felt like a jerk over what happened last night made me realize that she wanted it as bad as I did. I'd firmly believed I'd pushed myself on her. After she left without saying a word, my concentration had been shot, and I'd closed up shop. Drove home frustrated and horny, going over what happened between Bryn and me over and over again, trying to figure out how exactly how I let it happen. That kiss. Pulling Bryn into my arms. Touching her.

Yeah. A huge mistake, not one I can forget easily either.

It had been tremendously hard having to face her this morning, though somehow she made it easier on me by appearing in a beige outfit again, hardly looking at me, like I scared her. This Bryn I knew and understood, or so I thought. I'd been dealing with wallpaper Bryn for months and I was used to her like this.

It's gorgeous, elegant, sexy-as-fuck Bryn that does me in and makes my head spin. Not only does she look amazing, but she becomes bolder with the stylish clothes and the beautiful hair. She moves with confidence, looks me in the eye, talks to me.

Seeing her this morning in her usual beige getup tripped me up but only momentarily. Hearing her voice, watching her, and all I saw was the real woman behind the facade. She can hide all she wants in drab colors and severe hairstyles; I know who she is beneath the surface.

And I want more despite wanting to do the right thing.

She confuses me. I thought by pushing her away, it would solve all my problems. Instead, I feel like I have a whole bunch more.

Moving away from where Ivy and Bryn are still talking, I head toward my car and take off, going to my last quick appointment for the day, a meeting at my local bank with a possible investor.

My cell rings not two minutes after I pull out of the winery's parking lot and I check the screen to see it's my father. Speak of the devil. It's like the old man could sense someone was talking about him, thinking about him. Against my better judgment, I answer it—best to face him now than prolong it and have him harassing me tomorrow.

"Son." Vinnie's voice booms through the speakers of my car since I have my phone on Bluetooth. "It's been a long time."

He always acts like there's no reason we haven't spoken for months. "What's going on?" I ask, cutting right to the point.

"Ah, you're always full of the kindness for your old man, aren't you?" Vinnie chuckles, and I grit my teeth, wanting to hang up on him so bad it's killing me. "So I hear your fancy winery is having its reopening tomorrow."

"It sure is." He's never shown one iota of interest in the winery other than when I told him I bought it, and he said "that's nice" in his usual distracted, completely self-absorbed voice.

We never discussed it again.

"I was hoping I could get an invite."

Unease slips down my spine, and I clear my throat. "I thought you were more of a hard liquor fan," I say, trying to sound like I'm joking.

"Well, I'm not a big drinker of wine, I agree, but I want to be there when my only son shows off his new winery. It's going to be a proud moment, I'm sure."

A proud moment I absolutely one hundred percent don't want him to be a part of. "Are you sure you want to come? It'll be boring. Hardly anyone there that you know besides my friends."

"Anyone from baseball?" he asks.

Yeah. A few people, and I definitely don't want him around them. He tends to get in heated arguments whenever they discuss baseball and specifically his past in both the game and the league.

But shit, how can I refuse him? He's my father.

"A small handful but not a lot," I tell him, keeping my gaze focused on the road ahead of me. I hadn't even bothered sending him an invitation for tomorrow. I wonder if he's pissed. I wonder if this is some strange way for him to get revenge on me for ignoring him.

I wouldn't put it past my father. He's just that type of guy.

"I saw a write up in the paper," he explains. He still lives in the Bay Area, having been born and raised there. We were both lucky to be included in professional teams close to where we grew up. My dad always attributed it to the DeLuca curse—an apt word considering how crappy both of our pro careers became. "And realized this was going down tomorrow. I won't be able to attend the day events—I saw you're doing a tour and a wine tasting and all that good stuff—but I'd love to show up at the party tomorrow night if you'll have me."

"That can be arranged," I say, regret filling me in an instant. I hope this isn't a mistake.

"Great, good! I can't wait to see you. It's been far too long, son. I miss you."

Yeah, right. "It'll be good to see you too, but you do understand I'm going to be busy the entire night and won't have much time for miscellaneous chitchat." I won't have much time for his calculated reminiscing over our sometimes troubled past either. He loves to do that too and push me into a guilt spiral.

Our relationship is twenty levels of fucked up, I swear.

"I understand completely," he assures me. "I'll just be there basking in your glory, always the proud father. I won't disrupt your little party tomorrow night, I promise. Don't worry about me."

That he's describing tomorrow's event as "my little party" already sets me on edge, the asshole. I swear he says those sorts of things on purpose. I don't believe a word he says.

And I hate that I feel this way.

After he hangs up, I ponder over how I can handle the problem that is my father. I wonder if Bryn would help me. But if I set Bryn in my dad's sights, he'll probably try and make a pass and she'll end up beyond insulted.

Yeah. That's a risk I really don't want to take. Do I have a choice though? It's like my dad needs a babysitter and only a specialized few will do.

Still, I definitely don't want to subject Bryn to my rude bastard of a father.

Chapter Six

Matt

"THE PLACE LOOKS fabulous, man." Archer slaps me on the back so hard, I take a step forward, wincing when pain shoots through my knee. It still hurts. It'll always hurt. "You pulled it off. I bet everybody will have DeLuca Winery falling from their lips come tomorrow."

"Thanks, but the party only just started," I say, ever the grim reaper as I worry about anything and everything. The grounds are crowded with people, the lot filled with cars, including the dirt field we opened up specifically for the event.

My father still hasn't arrived which worries the shit out of me, but I can't sweat it. Maybe he'll never come at all. I figure I won't be that lucky. He knows how to put a damper on any party, big or small.

The image of my father crashing into the party, loud and drunk and making me look like a fool has set me on edge. I need to do something to take that edge off and quick.

"You're all gloom and doom today, asshole. Perk up. Life is good," Gage says, saluting me with his glass before he takes a swallow of a DeLuca Cabernet.

"Don't be so mean," Marina chastises as she slips her arm through Gage's. "It's an amazing party, Matt. I know everyone's impressed."

"Thanks, Marina." Her words mean a lot to me since she comes from one of the oldest families in the area. If anyone knows what's going on in the Napa Valley, it's Marina Knight. That I can impress her and she hears nothing but good things from those she knows, lets me breathe easier.

A little bit easier, at least.

My name is on the label, on the sign out front, on the building. It's a surreal feeling, finally seeing the fruition of months and months of hard labor, sweat, and tears.

The day's events came off without a hitch. The tour was a success, heavily attended by many, including plenty of local media. The wine tasting had been a nerve-wracking experience but soon turned into complete relief. Almost everyone enjoyed what they sampled, though there had been a few naysayers, but that was to be expected.

Bryn led the tasting, composed and elegant and thoughtful and amusing. She'd enraptured everyone, talking so enthusiastically about the wine and the DeLuca name and what it's going to mean to the Napa Valley in the coming years. Hell, even I believed my own hype.

She'd been utter perfection, and I never got a chance

to thank or praise her. I still haven't seen her arrive tonight and that surprised me. I figured she'd be here already.

I need her to be here already.

Gage and Marina head for one of food tables, and I glance around, checking out the crowd. I notice that the small live band is tuning up and getting ready to play. The weather tonight is perfect, not too cold, though I have outdoor heaters going on low to fill the air with warmth. There's a gentle breeze rustling the majestic oaks that are all over the property. White lights are strung in the trees surrounding the courtyard, illuminating the party without being too bright. There are bars set up on each corner of the courtyard, and they all have long lines, everyone wanting a glass of one of the new DeLuca wines. Servers move through the crowds with their trays, offering appetizers or flutes of sparkling wine.

It has all come together so perfectly, and I owe a lot of that to Bryn. But where is she?

"Matt! Your party is fabulous." Ivy comes at me, her pregnant belly so obvious it's preceding her. Archer stands at her side as she comes for me, enveloping me in a perfume-scented hug. "I can't believe how beautiful everything looks. Where's Bryn? I wanted to praise her too. I know she's done so much for you."

"She has. And you've done an amazing job too you know." I kiss her cheek before I let her go, thankful for all her decorating input. Everything looks freaking amazing because of her. Her design skills and expertise were just what I needed to ensure the grounds and the interiors looked modern yet stayed true to the authenticity of the winery in times past.

"I'm so glad you like it." She smiles, then notices Marina and Gage waiting in line. "I'll be right back. I want to talk to Marina."

Archer and I watch her go before Archer turns to me, a knowing smile on his smug-as-hell face. "Been diddling the help yet?"

Unease slips down my spine. "What the hell are you talking about?"

"Ah, don't pretend with me. I know your assistant has the hots for you, and I hear the feeling's mutual." Archer takes a sip from his glass. "Ivy talks. Her and your Miss James have become awfully close."

"What did Ivy tell you?" No way did Bryn tell Ivy about what happened a few nights ago, when I kissed her then pushed her away.

"Not a whole hell of a lot. Just that the two of you have been circling around each other in the office for far too long and that Bryn finally got herself a new wardrobe and some courage. I hear the dress she's wearing tonight is a plan to knock you completely on your ass with lust for her," Archer warns.

I swallow hard. Great. So she's going to be wearing a dress that makes her look like utter perfection? I can withstand that. No problem.

Shit, I hope I can.

She hadn't worn an uninspired beige outfit earlier today, and I was thankful for it, though she impressed me so damn much I probably wouldn't have even noticed.

She'd shown up dressed to perfection in a fitted deep purple dress, her hair pulled back into a sleek ponytail that wasn't so severe as her usual hairstyle. She'd looked beautiful. Assured and elegant, she was a fine representative of the DeLuca Winery.

"She's my assistant, nothing else," I tell Archer, needing to convince myself as well. "I know you've seen the pictures of when she got the makeover and you've given me endless shit, but I can't do anything about it. She works for me. I won't risk anything between us for fear it could go horribly wrong in an instant. She could turn against me and ruin my ass. Get me on sexual harassment charges or whatever."

"Oh, I get it. Tell that to Ivy though, since she's still hell bent on getting the two of you together," Archer says, his gaze roaming lazily over the crowd much as mine had only a few moments ago. "Hey, isn't that her? Your Bryn?"

I jerk my gaze to where Archer's staring, and I do a double take, my eyes widening when I see her.

Damn, she's . . . unbelievably gorgeous. I thought she was hot when she showed up in that black printed dress on Monday but right now, she's just fucking beautiful. There are no other words for it.

"That's her," I say, watching as she walks the far parameter of the courtyard, her head turning this way and that as she seemingly takes everything in. A small smile curves her plum-colored lips and she pushes her long, inky colored hair over her shoulder, stopping to talk to someone, laughing at whatever he said before she pats the man on the shoulder and keeps moving.

Jealousy moves through me, and I tell myself to knock it off. She can look at and talk to other people, especially if we're not together. Hell, even if we were together, I have no right to tell her what to do or who she talks to.

But I'd like that right. I sound like a complete Neanderthal but damn it, I want Bryn to be mine.

Still.

"She's a fucking looker man," Archer utters. "I'd get it if you gave up the million bucks for a piece of that."

Fury burns through my blood, and I glare at Archer. "Don't talk about her like that, you bastard. You could at least show the woman some respect," I tell him, my voice like steel.

"Ah, don't get your panties all twisted," Archer says, smiling as he shakes his head. "I love how caveman we all get when we're with the women we love."

"I never said I was in love with Bryn." I've worked with her for six months and have only just noticed her as a woman, though her scent has been driving me crazy pretty much since day one. But there's absolutely no way I'm in love with her. It's way too freaking soon for that.

I can't deny that I'm attracted to her though. Ever since that kiss, I can't stop remembering what she tastes like—how she felt in my arms.

"Yeah, well you're looking at her like you want to lick her from head to toe." Archer laughs when I glare at him. He cut too close to the truth. "See? You like her, DeLuca. It's okay. You can admit it. And as soon as the two of you fall into bed together, make sure you let us know so we can rescind the bet and let it die a happy, empty death."

"Hell, no. I'm going to win that bet, no matter what," I say with utter conviction.

"Keep dreaming," Archer says, clapping me on the back much like Gage had done earlier. Only this time, I keep my footing. "It's about damn time we see you show some interest in a girl. You've been celibate for far too long."

I don't even notice when Archer moves away from me. I keep my gaze locked on Bryn as she moves through the crowd, crossing the courtyard, seemingly coming right for me. The dress she's wearing fits her like a dream. A daringly bold magenta color, it stands out in the crowd of mostly black. The silky fabric clings lovingly to her breasts and hips. Her shoulders are exposed, the straps are thin and the skirt ends just above her knee in a gentle flare.

The color is beautiful on her, bringing out the flush in her cheeks. Her hair is done: long, wavy black-as-midnight locks. She spots me and a secretive little smile curves her lush lips as she approaches on silvery colored stiletto sandals that shimmer in the light.

She looks like a fucking fairy princess brought to me just for this night. I'm tempted to take her hand, say screw the party and find somewhere private where we can be alone and naked together.

What the hell is wrong with you?

Bryn James. That's what the hell is wrong with me. The problem? I like this problem. Hell, I'm reveling in it. I shouldn't want her, but I do. I shouldn't think about her in this manner but I can't stop. Hell, I even dream about her.

Sweaty, wicked dreams that leave me aching for her every time I wake.

"Sorry I'm late," she says stopping in front of me. Her scent carries on the breeze, deliciously sweet, and I inhale as discreetly as possible. My dick twitches, and I will it down. Now is absolutely not the time, but it has other plans, every one of them involving me and Bryn and the two of us naked. "I had to get home and change real quick, and traffic was a nightmare getting back out here."

"You haven't missed much," I tell her, letting my gaze blatantly roam over her before it settles on her chest. All that exposed skin is a fucking distraction. "You look amazing."

The smile grows and my body tightens in reaction. "So do you."

I'm wearing a suit, and I'm as uncomfortable as ever, but I'll take her compliment. "Thanks. Did I tell you I thought you did a fantastic job earlier at the wine tasting?"

"Oh really? No, we never talked, and I was sort of nervous over it all." Her gaze grows earnest as she watches me. "You really thought I did a good job?" She sounds surprised at my praise. Doesn't she realize her worth, both to the business and . . . to me?

Maybe not.

"You led the group expertly and spoke so highly of the winery. You were perfect." I smile, fighting to the urge to touch her.

Relief crosses her face. "Whew. Thank God. I really was worried."

"I don't know why. You were composed and handled

yourself well. I honestly don't think you could ever disappoint me," I say before I can stop myself.

Her expression softens, her eyes sparkling with some unknown emotion. Christ, she's gorgeous and sweet and reminding me of that night when I not-so-accidentally kissed her. "Thank you, Matt. That means a lot to me, that you would say that." She pauses, her gaze tearing from mine so she can watch the party unfold before us. "You've done such a fabulous job of putting this all together. Everything looks so beautiful."

"It does look good, doesn't it? And you had plenty to do with putting this together as well, you know." I glance around, pride suffusing me. Everyone definitely looks like they're enjoying themselves. But we still have hours to go.

"Hard to believe the day is almost over," she says, sinking her teeth into her lower lip as she turns her gaze on me once more.

Hell. I want to grab her again. Kiss her until she can't see straight, until *I* can't freaking see straight. Having her here standing by my side, wearing a dress that should probably be illegal is pushing me past my limits.

I want to get her alone. Now.

Really?

Really.

"Do you mind coming with me to my office real quick?" I ask, my brain scrambling for an excuse. I shouldn't do this. Shouldn't ditch the party; the most important night of my life.

A night that could be ruined if my father does show and does something stupid which he's an expert at.

She frowns. "What for?"

"I forgot something in there, and I need your help to find it." Lame as hell, but I don't care. I'm filled with the need to be with her. Alone. Just for a moment.

"Um, okay. Do you think it's smart for the both of us to leave the party at the same time?" Bryn looks unsure, but I can't let that bother me now.

Taking her hand, I lead her toward the office building, savoring how her fingers clasp mine. "It'll only be for a few minutes. Besides, there are other employees out mingling, and Archer loves to keep an eye on everything."

Bryn doesn't reply.

We enter the building, though I don't bother turning on the lights; the countless strands of lights outside illuminate the interior well enough. I take Bryn to my office, letting go of her hand when we enter.

"What exactly are you looking for you so I can help you?" she asks.

Guilt gnaws at me for the ruse, but I push it aside. Fuck it. "I didn't lose anything, Bryn. I just . . . wanted to get you alone."

She parts her lips as she stares at me but doesn't say a word.

Her silence prompts me to go for it.

Finally.

Bryn

"I SHOULDN'T DO this." Matt says, coming right at me, one determined step after another, and I slowly start to back up, fear and excitement bubbling up inside me, making it hard to think clearly.

"Shouldn't do what?" I lift my chin, my gaze meeting his, and I can see all the turbulent, confusing emotions in his eyes, the grim set of his jaw and usually lush mouth. The man means business, what sort of business I'm not exactly sure, but I can take a guess. Increasing my pace, I take hurried backward steps to get away from all that handsome intensity coming at me until my butt meets the wall.

I'm trapped. And in the best possible place too.

In his office, alone with him and in the dark, right back where we started.

"You've been driving me fucking crazy since the minute you arrived tonight," he practically growls, stopping just in front of me.

I have? I want to ask, but I keep my lips clamped tight. I only just got here and besides, he never seems to notice me, not that I really want him to now. Not after the fiasco that went down a few nights ago.

Or at least, that's what I tell myself.

"I don't understand how I could be, considering I just got here," I say, panic flaring within me when his eyes darken.

Do I want this? I try so hard to earn his respect and I let myself end up in these dangerous situations. I'm beyond confused. I want my boss to value me as an employee, but I also want him to see *me*. Really see me. Not just as the dependable, efficiently organized Miss James who makes his life so much easier.

I want Matt to see me as a woman. A woman he wants.

For one shining moment, he did. It ended disastrously, but here I am, alone with him yet again.

Playing with fire.

The thought floating through my brain is apt, considering the potent heat in Matt's gaze.

"Trust me. You're a distraction I absolutely do not need," he says, his voice low. Sexy.

A tremble moves through me, but I stand my ground. "I've done nothing but work my tail off for you the entire day, so please don't tell me you're suddenly angry with me now," I retort, wincing the moment the words leave me. I blame my mounting frustration over our ridiculous situation. The push and pull is getting old, and I'm not sure I can take it much longer.

I'm tired, I've done nothing but live and breathe this winery reopening for the last few weeks if not months, and I'm ready to go home and crawl into bed when I've only just arrived here. Pull the covers over my head and sleep for a month.

But if a certain someone wanted to join me in my bed, there wouldn't be any sleeping involved—just plenty of nakedness and kissing and hot, delicious sex.

My entire body flushes at the thought.

"And I appreciate you working that pretty tail of yours off for me, Bryn, really I do," he drawls, his gaze dropping low. Like he's actually trying to check out my backside. His flirtatious tone shocks me, rendering me still.

Our relationship isn't like this. Strictly professional is how we've kept it, minus the one incident we haven't really talked about. I can still taste his lips on mine, not that I'd ever bring it up now.

His last remark though was most definitely what I would consider flirting. And the way he's looking at me . . .

Oh. My.

My cheeks warm when he stops directly in front of me. I can feel his body heat, smell his intoxicating scent, and I press my lips together to keep from saying something really stupid.

God, I want you. So bad my entire body aches for your touch.

Yeah. Again I sound like those romance novels. The ones I used to find on my grandma's bedside table when I was young. I always thought those emotions were so exaggerated. No way could that actually occur in real life.

But I'm feeling it. Right now. Again. With Matthew DeLuca. And the way he's looking at me makes me think he's feeling it too.

"So um, h-how have I been driving you crazy?" I swallow hard. I sound like a stuttering idiot, and I'm trying to calm my racing heart but it's no use. We're staring at each other in silence, the only sound is our accelerated breathing, and then he reaches out. Rests his fingers against my cheek. Lets them drift along my face.

Slowly I close my eyes and part my lips, sharp pleasure piercing through me at his intimate touch. I curl my fingers against the wall as if I can grab onto it, afraid I might slide to the ground if I don't get a grip and soon.

I can smell him. Feel him. We've been close to each

other before but not like this. Never like this. The first time was an accident and had turned into an opportunity—a rushed opportunity that had ultimately ended in utter disappointment.

I don't want to risk that again. I don't know if I could survive it again.

But I want it. I want him.

"You look so damn beautiful tonight," he whispers, his rough voice sending a scatter of goose bumps across my skin.

"Thank you," I say because I don't know what else to do. I crack my eyes open to find he's moved even closer, one hand braced against the wall, the other still touching my face. Tilting my head back, I meet his gaze, my lids flickering when he strokes his thumb across my lower lip.

"It's taking everything inside of me not to just give in and kiss you," he admits gruffly, his hot eyes roaming over my face, then dropping lower, settling on my chest. I can feel my nipples tighten beneath the silk fabric of my dress and I'm suddenly achingly aware of what little clothing I'm wearing. No bra, no panties . . .

My dress is the only barrier between Matt's hands and my skin.

God, I want that. I do. I want to feel his hands roam all over me. I want his mouth on mine; I want his mouth everywhere. I'm tired of resisting him, especially when he so clearly wants me as much as I want him.

For once, I'm going to be bold. I want to see what he does when I invite him to do exactly what he wants to me.

"What's stopping you? We've already kissed before." I reach out, slip my fingers down the length of his black tie. I can't believe I just said that. I can't believe I'm touching him though really I'm only caressing his tie. Big deal.

But I can feel all that hot, hard strength beneath his shirt, the beat of his heart, the scent of his skin. Relief floods me. We've been dancing around this attraction, especially the last few days, and it feels like we're finally giving in. Again.

Well, I've been dancing around it. He always seemed mostly oblivious to me.

Maybe he isn't. If his current behavior is any indication, he definitely isn't.

"*I'm* stopping me. Or at least I should be," he says, resting both of his hands on my waist as he steps so close, our legs tangle, our chests brush. I hold my breath, waiting for what I know will be a totally disappointing conclusion to our conversation.

He doesn't say anything at all. Instead, he lowers his head, his mouth settling on mine, softly. Sweetly. His kiss obliterates everything, all of my thoughts and worries and concerns, until I'm consumed by the sound and the feel and the smell of him. He surrounds me, overwhelms me, and when he thrusts his tongue deep inside my mouth, I'm lost.

And only Matt will be able to find me.

When he breaks the kiss to slide his mouth down the length of my neck, his low, sexy growl makes my insides flutter. He sounds like he's barely keeping himself in control, and I reach out, wrapping my arms around his neck, burying my fingers in his hair like I enjoy doing. His hair is so thick and soft, the strands cling to my fingers, and I feel like I can't get enough of him.

The way he's kissing me makes me think he can't get enough of me either. His mouth returns to mine and devours me. The kiss so hot, wet, and deep, I feel completely and utterly consumed.

I love it. I want more. I cling to him, mold my body to his and wish he would slip his hands beneath my dress. I want to witness his discovery that I'm wearing no bra, no panties, no nothing beneath it.

I have a feeling he'd be rather pleased with that revelation.

"Jesus, Bryn, you feel good," he says when we come up for air. His hand is roaming, rising from where it rests on my waist to slide up, over my ribcage to rest just beneath my breast. He pulls away slightly, catching sight of my nipples pebbling painfully beneath the silky fabric of my dress, and he lifts his other hand. Traces the deep V neckline of my dress with his fingertip, his touch feather-light as he brushes my skin, causing skitters to rush across it.

Sighing, I close my eyes, savoring his bold, yet delicate touch. He slips his hand beneath the fabric, covering my right breast with just his fingers and makes a rough sound of pleasure at finding me braless.

His calloused fingers play with my nipple, driving me crazy with need, and I drop my arms from around his neck, arching into his touch as I keep my eyes tightly closed. I'm almost afraid to look at him for fear he'll abandon me once he realizes what we're doing.

And then he's kissing me yet again, his hands moving up to cup my face, holding me still. I want to melt. His thumbs brush across my cheeks, his touch gentle, the way he cups my face almost as if he . . . cherishes me. No man has ever held me like this, kissed me like this before. I wrap my arms around his waist, clinging to him, whispering against his lips *please don't stop, don't ever stop*, when he stills. Lifts his head from mine and cocks his ear toward the window.

"Did you hear that?" he asks, his voice hushed.

Beyond the roaring in my ears brought on by his skilled mouth and my own pleading words, I can't really hear anything. Oh, there's the partygoers outside, their chatter a low hum in the quiet confines of his office. A hint of music coming from the hired band but that's it.

"I swear I heard someone yell my name." He kisses the tip of my nose, one cheek, then the other. "Sounded like my father," he whispers.

"Really?" He kisses my forehead, my temple, my ear, my chin. Sweet, soft little kisses that make my lips tingle in anticipation. "I didn't realize he was coming."

"I forgot to tell you about it." He kisses me this time, his lips lingering on mine for long, delicious moments before he finally breaks it. "I didn't think he'd show up. More like I hoped he wouldn't show up."

I'm surprised that he would even invite him. Last I heard from Ivy, their relationship was strained at best.

And then I hear it. A loud, rough bellow:

"Matthew DeLuca, where the fuck are you, son?"

Matt hears it too—who couldn't? His entire body goes

still and he pulls away, leaving me. I'm immediately cold without him near.

"That's him," he says grimly. "I should go."

"I'll go with you. Do you want my help?" I reach for him, but he's still backing up, pulling completely away from my grip.

He's withdrawing into himself right before me, and I hate seeing it, though I can't blame him.

He needs to go subdue his father and quick.

"Just mingle and make sure everyone's having a good time. I need to go and make sure he doesn't make an ass out of himself and me and ruin everything," Matt mutters before he turns tail and flees.

I slump against the wall, my heart thumping wildly, my lips still tingling from his delicious kisses. I need to compose myself. Gather my thoughts and emotions and put on the hostess mask.

I need to help Matt. He's stressed. The last thing he needs to deal with is his volatile father making a scene.

Putting aside my tumultuous emotions and locking my still-wobbly knees, I stand up straight, smooth my hands over my skirt and head for the courtyard.

Chapter Seven

Matt

"SON! THERE YOU are. I've been looking everywhere for you," my father says as he stumbles toward me.

"Well, you found me." I grab hold of my dad's arm to keep him steady. Smells like someone already hit up a bar before arriving here and disgust fills me. I'm pissed that he would show up to one of the most important nights of my life and my career, drunk as hell.

But what did I expect? Not like he cares about me, or my reputation; he's such a selfish old bastard.

"Where's the wine?" he asks loudly, drawing the attention of more than one partygoer. "I want a sample of that shit you're brewing."

He can't even get the terms right. "I think you should lay off the booze for a while," I say as I try and steer him toward the table laden with food. He needs to eat something and drink some black coffee, anything to soak up all that alcohol coursing through his system and sober him up somewhat.

"Don't tell me what to do." He jerks his arm out of my hold and heads toward the table I wanted him to go to in the first place, grabs a small plate and starts loading up on endless appetizers.

I follow after him, keeping close, smiling and chatting with everyone I recognize or know. I feel like I can't leave my father's side, which is such total bullshit, especially because I had to leave a perfectly willing woman back in my office.

Not that I should've been fooling around with a woman in my office when I had a party going on out here but . . .

My mind drifts to Bryn and how good she'd felt in my arms. I'd had my hand beneath her dress only moments ago, touching her breast, playing with her nipple, and she hadn't protested. No, she'd arched into my touch, little sounds of pleasure escaping her. She looked amazing in that dress, her long hair down, her lips parted as she gasped when I gently pinched.

Hell. I want more. I wanted to take her back to my place, strip her out of that dress and kiss every inch of her naked skin. Instead, I'm babysitting my drunken dad.

Fuck, life is really unfair sometimes.

"Quite the spread you got here," Dad says, clutching his already overflowing plate. "How much did this cost you anyway?"

Damn it, I want to die of embarrassment, his voice is so loud. "Don't worry Dad, I have it under control," I reassure him.

"Little snot, won't tell me how much money you're spending on this fancy, good-for-nothing shindig. Not that it matters. I don't care what you do with your money. I already gave you your piece of my pie but that's it. I'm cutting you off. You'll have to earn everything else, fair and square." He lurches toward me, his plate nearly goes flying, and I take it from him, wait while he readjusts himself and stands up straighter.

White hot anger flows through my veins, setting my blood on fire. I want to kill him. Wrap my hands around his neck and squeeze until he's not breathing any longer. Not that I could do such a thing, but every time he acts like this, which is pretty much every time I see him, he makes me hate him more.

It's a lot more complicated than that though, my relationship with my dad. I also love him. Still seek out his approval despite how much trouble he causes.

And Vinnie DeLuca causes an enormous amount of trouble everywhere he goes.

"Let's find you somewhere to sit," I tell my dad, grabbing hold of his arm again and leading him toward the tables where guests sit and eat. He jerks against my hold, muttering a string of curse words in protest, but I ignore him. The old man might be the same size as me, but I'm younger and stronger.

"You're manhandling me like you're gonna kick me out of here, son," he says when I push him into a seat. Thank God this table is empty. I don't need him spouting off to other guests.

"Just trying to help you out, Dad," I say through my

clenched teeth. Glancing around, I check to see if anyone is watching, specifically anyone from the media, but for the most part, no one's acknowledging us.

Thank God.

"Mr. DeLuca! It's a pleasure meeting you." Bryn appears in front of the table, an angel in magenta clutching a white coffee mug. The smile on her face is as bright as her eyes, and she shoots me a knowing look before she returns her attention to my father.

"Well, well, who's this pretty young thing?" Dad takes the mug from her and sips, wincing when he discovers what it is. "Coffee?"

"Decaf. And laced with whiskey." She winks at him, then winks at me, and I know she's full of absolute crap, just saying that to make him happy. God, I could hug her for this. Kiss her.

Not that I need an excuse to kiss Bryn. My body is still humming from our shared kisses.

"Thank you," Dad says gratefully as he drinks from the cup, finishing off half of it in a couple of swallows. "It's good."

"Miss James is notorious for making the best cup of coffee around," I say, hoping she can hear the gratitude in my voice.

"You know her, son?"

"She's my assistant." I wave a hand between them. "Dad, this is Bryn James. Bryn, this is Vinnie DeLuca."

"Lovely meeting you." She takes Dad's proffered hand, literally batting her eyelashes at him. I swear I hear a hint of her Texas twang when she speaks.

And it's sexy as hell.

"Likewise." Dad won't let go of her hand, and she has to tug out of his hold as discreetly as possible, not that he notices. "You're a looker, darlin'. Where you from?"

"Why, Cactus, Texas, sir." More batting of the eyelashes, her voice is syrupy thick with the accent. She's flirting with my dad and I don't know if I should be horrified or thankful.

She doesn't really . . . *want* to flirt with him, does she?

"Well, what do you know, I met a hot little thing who lived near Cactus years ago, when I was on one of the farm teams. That was a long, long time ago though." Dad grins, most likely reliving the memory and enjoying the hell out of it.

"I probably know her. Not many people ever leave Cactus," she says.

"Miss James, can I speak with you for a moment? Privately?" I rest my hand on Dad's shoulder. "You'll be all right alone so you can eat, right Dad?"

"Of course. Go handle your business with your Miss James." Dad waves a hand, cackling wickedly. "You sure are smart son, more than I give you credit for, hiring a looker like this one. I bet you chase her around your desk all the damn time, trying to get your hands on that ass. I know I would."

Bryn stiffens, her expression frozen with shock. I see it happen right before my eyes. She looks at me, her gaze a little wild, her chest rising and falling with her accelerated breaths.

I have no idea why his words triggered that strong of a

reaction, but, of course, my dad's involved so what else is new? The man offends women—everyone—on a constant basis.

"Dad. Come on. Show the lady some respect," I say, giving his shoulder a firm squeeze.

"Yeah, yeah." Dad starts digging into his food, not bothering to offer her an apology, and I feel like shit.

This night is going from bad to worse at a rapid pace.

Bryn

MATT STEERS ME to a dark corner a few feet away from the packed courtyard so we're standing beneath a mighty oak that actually doesn't have a string of lights wound through the branches. His expression is grim, his gaze contrite as he turns to face me.

"I'm sorry." He runs a hand over his face, looking downright traumatized. "My father is an asshole, and I can't believe he said those things to you."

"It's okay," I say softly, my heart still panging from Vinnie DeLuca's earlier words. They'd cut way too close to the truth, reminding me of my old boss.

And of how I haven't changed a bit, even though I think I have. I fall into the same habits time and again, self-destructive to the point that I'm wondering if I seek this sort of attention out.

Was I so neglected as a child that I prefer any attention, good or bad?

"No, it's not okay. You came sweeping in, handling everything perfectly and he still treats you like that. He's awful." Matt blows out a frustrated breath and rests his hands on his hips, staring out at the courtyard. The music has picked up the pace, and people are actually dancing. The wine is flowing and being praised; the grounds are still packed with people. The party is a huge success.

And here Matt stands, looking so desolate and sad all I can think about is how much I want to comfort him.

Don't do it, Bryn. Not in public. He'll probably freak.

Ignoring my inner voice's protestations, I step closer to him and rest my hand on his chest. I can feel his heart pumping wildly beneath my palm, and I smile up at him, trying to offer reassurance. "He's an old man stuck in his ways. Do you know how many of those types live in Cactus?"

He smiles. "I did notice you slipped into your Texan accent when you spoke to him."

"I did? I didn't even notice." I smooth my fingers down the length of Matt's tie, loving how firm and solid he feels beneath my touch. I wish I could see him naked. I know he has a body to die for. I've seen him bare-chested and sexy as hell online, but I'd prefer to see the real thing. So I can get my hands all over his hot, hard flesh.

"I appreciate you trying to help me," he says, his voice low and sexy, igniting that flicker of desire that always seems to burn within me when he's near into a full-on flame. "You were great with him. Even when he started insulting you."

A soft huff of laughter escapes me. "I know how to handle guys like your father. I've dealt with them a lot." Too much. It's like I can't ever escape them.

He steps away from me, and I drop my hand, pushing aside the sadness that nips at me. I'm acting like a girlfriend when I need to remember my place. I work for him. I'm his assistant.

That's it.

"I'll ask Archer or Gage to spend time with him for a while and keep him entertained," Matt says, his mouth grim. "They know how to handle him. They have before."

"I can do it," I say, wincing the moment the words leave me. Why did I volunteer myself to sit with Vinnie DeLuca? Am I crazy?

Yes, crazy for your boss and looking for any way to please him.

"No way." He shakes his head, but I can see it in his eyes. He's desperate. And I if I can ease his stress by babysitting his dad, then so be it.

Even though I'm totally taking a chance here. From what I can see in just the few minutes I've spent in Vinnie's company, he's beyond obnoxious.

"I can handle your father. I'm a lot tougher than I look," I say, wanting him to agree so I can prove I can handle anything he throws my way.

"I don't know . . ." He rubs his chin, his gaze full of doubt.

"Let me do this for you," I whisper, swallowing hard the moment the words leave me. Why do I want to please him so bad?

Because you like him, silly.

A sigh escapes him and he shakes his head. "Listen, if he's rude to you or gets out of control, find me, and I'll take care of him. I'll keep my eyes on you too and make sure he doesn't try anything crazy." He studies me, just waiting for me to bail on him I'm sure.

But I won't. I'm doing this—for him.

"He'll be fine. And I don't mind. Really." Well, I sort of do, but I'll do anything to ease Matt's burden, especially tonight. "I can sit with him, hopefully sober him up and maybe convince him to leave? Is that what you'd prefer?"

I see the guilt and the worry swirling in the brown depths of his gaze. I get it. My grandma is crazy. I adore her, but I wouldn't want her out in public with me, especially on a night as big as this. She'd embarrass the hell out of me.

"Yeah. Actually, I would. I sound like an ass, wanting to get rid of my dad, but if you can subdue him and somehow convince him he needs to go, that would be perfect," he finally says.

"I'll do what I can." I turn and start to head back to the table where Vinnie is sitting when Matt grabs my hand and tugs me back toward him.

"Thank you." He lifts my hand and presses a soft, damp kiss to the back of it. My knees wobble when I see the glow in Matt's gaze as he studies me. "For everything."

"Y-you're w-welcome," I stutter. I can hardly think when he's touching me, looking like he wants to devour me, let alone talking to him. No man has ever made me feel quite like this before.

"We'll talk in a bit, all right? I need to socialize and schmooze," he says as he slowly releases my hand.

"Fine. Makes sense. I've heard nothing but good

things from everyone I've talked to, I promise. DeLuca Winery is a big hit." I offer him a quick smile before I flee, going to the table where Vinnie sits munching on one appetizer after another. He spots me, his eyes lighting up, and he pats the empty chair beside him.

"Come sit by me, girly. Want a glass of wine? Some food?" He pushes his plate toward me like he's going to share it as I sit down next to him.

"No, thank you," I say, laying on the sweetness. May as well play it up and entertain the old booger for a while. The last thing I want to do is drink with the already drunk Vinnie, and I'm not really hungry since nerves are still eating at my stomach.

"How long you work here for Matt?" Vinnie asks amicably.

"Well, I was working for the winery before Matt purchased it. I was the assistant of the other owner. We all thought we'd lost our jobs but then Matt asked us to attend a staff meeting. When he announced that he wanted to keep us all working for him, we were so grateful. We've been loyal to him ever since," I explain, remembering how big and strong and handsome I thought he looked that day. Sweeping in and making his grand declarations, and better yet? Actually keeping his word. I'd wanted to fall at his feet and weep in gratitude, I'd been so thankful.

And I know I wasn't the only one who felt that way either. Men who'd worked in the vineyard for the previous owner's family for years were incredibly thankful for Matt's generosity as well. It's why we all work so hard for him. He shows us respect, and we show it right back.

"That was a good thing my boy did," Vinnie says with a firm nod. "Keeping you all here working for him. Everyone loves my Matthew. Every once in a while, he has a bit of goodness in his heart."

"He's a good boss," I agree, wondering how his dad can both praise Matt and knock him down all in one sentence.

"Even though he don't know shit about wine," Vinnie mutters, making me stifle a laugh. "What? It's true and you know it, girly. I bet he's been scrambling since he bought this place trying to learn everything he can."

His dad wasn't too far off the mark with that assessment. "What he lacks in knowledge, he makes up for in enthusiasm."

"Now that was a diplomatic answer." Vinnie grins and points at me. "I can see why he kept you on. Not only do you look real good, you sound good too."

"Thank you. I think." I glance around, looking for Matt, and spot him standing with a group of people who seem to be enthusiastically chatting him up.

Good. He doesn't need the stress his dad brings him while worrying if anyone is impressed with the wine. Not that I ever doubted he'd succeed, but he's been on edge for days. Weeks. Months.

Probably why he kissed you. Needed an outlet for all that nervous energy and you were the perfect distraction.

The thought comes upon me so quickly, I go still as I turn it over again and again in my head. Could that really be the reason why he kissed me? A way to unleash all that edgy energy he's been living on for the last few weeks?

God, I hope not.

"So can I ask you a question, pretty lady?"

Vinnie's voice reminds me what I'm supposed to be doing, and I turn to look at him, a tentative smile on my face. "Sure. Go ahead."

"Are you fucking my son?"

Chapter Eight

Bryn

MY MOUTH IS completely dry as I gape at Matt's father, shocked that he would say such a crude and horrible thing.

They have similar features, Vinnie and Matt. Same dark hair and brown eyes, though Matt's are much kinder than Vinnie's cold, almost mocking glare. His mouth is set in a firm line too, as if he doesn't smile much.

I bet he doesn't. It seems he's got a mean streak in him a mile wide.

"Well? Cat got your tongue or what? I can only take your silence as confirmation that yes, indeedy, you're fucking my son," he says. "The lucky bastard."

Swallowing hard, I search for composure. The very last thing I want him to believe is that Matt and I are having some sort of illicit affair. I wouldn't put it past this man to sell the story to whoever would listen if it brought him any bit of attention.

"Your son is my boss," I finally say, my voice raspy, and I clear my throat. "That's it. There's nothing between us except a working relationship."

He casts a skeptical glance my way. "Uh huh. That's why he looks at you like you're his favorite dessert and he's a starving man. I get it. Really I do. I never could keep my dick in my pants, you know, especially when faced with a gorgeous woman such as yourself. And neither can he." Reaching out, he touches me, slides his fingers down my forearm. I yank my arm away, my skin literally crawling from his touch.

"There's nothing going on between us," I say, my voice firm, my insides anything but. I'm a nervous, quaking mess, afraid this man will somehow figure out that Matt and I have at least kissed.

His questions, his blunt wording, are tainting everything I've shared with Matt. Reminding me that I'm just the same ol' girl from Cactus, Texas. The girl everyone chases after and expects sexual favors from, all because she has a pretty face and curvy figure.

That's me. I'm that girl, the one that everyone makes feel like she's a slut. A whore. I've slept with two men in my life. I could count the sexual experiences I've had on one hand. Nothing lasting, nothing good, and I always run before it can turn into anything more. I'm always too scared.

Yet I'm the shameless hussy who's out to fuck around with every man I see. I'm a home wrecker. A man stealer. A girl who's good for nothing but cock sucking. A pervert's dream. I've been told this time and again.

And I'm being told it right now.

"You keep on saying there's nothing between you two but soon you'll fall under the DeLuca charm. You all do. We're irresistible. My son and I have both had plenty of women. I know when one's interested. And you my girl, you are definitely interested." Vinnie puts his hand over mine and holds firm, trapping it on the table. "If my son doesn't take the bait, just know I'm always here waiting whenever you're ready."

Oh my God. Now he thinks they're interchangeable? That I'll just bounce from father to son? "You're disgusting," I say, my voice low as I finally snatch my hand back from beneath his.

He laughs, the sound so loud more than a few people turn and look in our direction, including Matt. He shoots me a look of concern, but I shake my head, offer him a quick smile. The last thing I want is him coming over here and discovering this particular conversation. I can handle this man on my own.

He's not the first to think like this, and I'm guessing he won't be the last.

"Disgusting only because you don't want to hear the truth." He reaches for his cup of coffee and drains it. "Keep doing what you're doing, girly. He'll get you into his bed sooner or later."

That's it. I've had it. The man is a pig, and I need to get him out of here. "How did you get here tonight, Mr. DeLuca?" I ask, using my best, most professional voice. Not a twang or y'all in sight.

"Ah, now we're back to the formalities huh? Well, I

got myself a ride. The car and driver are sitting out in the parking lot," he says with a grin.

"Then let's go." I stand and grab hold of his arm, yanking him to his feet. He stares down at me in shock, most likely surprised little ol' me could tug him to his feet like that, but I just smile my best smile and lead him toward the entrance of the winery. "You need to get on home. I know Matt was thrilled you thought of him and wanted to stop by, but I think your time here is through."

"You can't just push me out of here," he mutters, but I ignore him practically dragging him by the arm toward the valets we hired for this evening. I paste my cordial, I-work-here smile on my face as I stop before them.

"We're looking for Mr. DeLuca's car. Do you happen to know where it is?"

One of them did, enabling me with the pleasure of dumping Vinnie DeLuca off onto some other poor, hapless soul and wiping my hands of him and his antics for the evening.

"Think you can get rid of me that quick, missy?" Vinnie shouts from the open window of his car, but I ignore him. Why engage the crazy?

I head back to the courtyard, wincing when my new stiletto sandals pinch my toes. I'm not used to heels or to walking on graveled pathways and cobbled courtyards *in* heels. I can't wait to soak my feet in the bath when I get home.

Alone.

Because there is no way I can pursue something, anything with Matt. Spending just ten minutes in his father's presence confirmed that. I can't go on pretending we would work out. I'd be seen as the gold-digging slut because I'm the poor girl from Texas dating the rich, billionaire boss and he'd be seen as the ass who couldn't keep it in his pants around his own employee.

Any sort of relationship between the two of us, temporary or serious, could ruin his reputation as a businessman in the area. I refuse to play a part in that. I would never be able to forgive myself.

And what would that do to me? I can't destroy my last chance here at a great job. If I fail at this, I'm going home. I can't afford to live in this outrageously expensive state while unemployed. Lord knows I'd hightail it out of here if I did end up parting ways with Matt professionally. It's hard enough as it is, finding a job that pays as well as mine in the area.

My footsteps slow, and I stop just at the edge of the courtyard, watching everyone. I see Gage and Marina out on the dance floor swaying in each other's arms as they smile and then laugh. I see Matt talking with another group, all of them men, every one of them reeking with importance.

I hope they can give him the connections he's looking for.

He looks so handsome in his dark suit and wine-colored tie, his hair ruffled by the occasional breeze. His smile flashes white against the tan of his skin and there are slight wrinkles around his eyes, as if he laughs often.

Which I hope he does. I haven't seen him laugh much since he's been so stressed-out since I started working for him, but hopefully that will change once everything settles down. Then he can relax and reap the benefits of all this hard work.

I probably won't be around to witness it though. And that thought alone fills me with such complete and utter sadness, I almost fall to the ground, my legs get so wobbly.

Pushing on, I head toward the crowds opposite of where Matt stands. I find an empty table and collapse in a chair, slipping my hand beneath the heavy weight of my hair, so I can rub my neck. No wonder I don't wear it down very often. It's heavy and thick, making me hot and my neck hurt.

I should just cut it all off and be done with it.

"Are you all right? You look like you're contemplating murder." Ivy pulls out a chair and settles in next to me.

"Only the murder of my hair." At her weird look I explain. "I'm thinking of cutting it all off."

"Don't you dare. It's gorgeous."

I shrug. "Like anyone notices. This has all been for nothing."

"Ah, Matt didn't notice? I know he's busy trying to keep everyone happy tonight," Ivy reminds me.

"Oh, he noticed." He definitely noticed if his mouth fused with mine and his hands roaming all over my body earlier was any indication. "His father came along though and ruined everything."

Ivy's mouth dropped open. "His father came? I never saw him."

"Aren't you lucky?" I mutter.

"Aw. Did he say something awful to you?" Ivy reaches out and grabs my hand, giving it a quick squeeze. "He's terrible—says the most offensive things ever. When I was younger, he used to try and hit on me."

"He doesn't try and hit on you now?"

"Well, I haven't seen him in a while and besides, Archer would kill him. Like tear him apart and murder him with his bare hands if he so much as leered at me, let alone touched me." Ivy smiles, a dreamy look in her eyes. "He's so hot when he gets all possessive like that."

Envy curls through me, gripping me tight. "Must be nice."

"Someday I bet you'll experience the same thing with Matt," Ivy says, full of a confidence I wished I felt even a tenth of.

Instead of making her more curious, I decide to put on a brave face. "Yeah, maybe I will," I say with a false enthusiasm that makes Ivy give me the side eye.

I can't get anything right, I swear.

Matt

I CAUGHT SIGHT of Bryn escorting my dad out of here not even twenty minutes ago, and it was like a weight had been lifted off me, making me infinitely lighter. It took everything in me not to fret and worry like a little old lady, my gaze constantly going to where Bryn sat with Dad.

I was afraid he'd say something horrible to her, or worse, touch her in an inappropriate manner. Wouldn't be the first time he's done something like that to some poor, innocent woman.

I just don't want him doing it to *my* woman.

With my dad off the premises, I find my focus and really start to work it. I talk to the local winery owners I invited, who all seemed grudgingly impressed with my wine list. I speak with plenty of local media who want to feature the DeLuca Winery; being a former pro ball player gives my story an extra edge they all want to explore.

I haven't eaten dinner and I'm starved, living on the occasional appetizer I find here and there, taking way too many swigs of wine. My head is spinning—I'm high on tonight's event coming together so perfectly—and I wonder where the hell Bryn is.

Plans to celebrate with her are definitely on my late-night agenda.

"Have you seen Bryn?" I ask Archer when I find him moving through the crowd, clutching two glasses, one full of water. I figure he's on his way back to Ivy.

"She's sitting with Ivy over there." He gestures with one of the glasses. "Ivy asked me to grab her a drink."

I should probably stay and talk with my guests some more, but I'm growing exhausted being on all the time. I need a break. I want to hang out with my people. "Yeah, I'll come with you."

"Uh huh." Archer flashes me a knowing smile over his shoulder as I fall into step behind him. "Missing your girl, hmm?"

"She's not my girl," I say, though the thought of Bryn with any other man, of her giving another man the right to call her his girl, fills me with a near overwhelming rush of jealousy.

Yeah. That was sort of a lie. I wouldn't mind if Bryn was my girl. But she can't be my girl. I have a bet to win.

Fuck the bet.

"You got what—less than forty days? Then she can be your girl. If you can hold out that long," Archer says, stopping at the table where Ivy and Bryn are sitting, deep in conversation. "Look who I found, ladies," he announces as he sets the glasses in front of the women.

They both glance up, their gazes dark and not necessarily happy when they see me.

Weird.

"Hey, Matt," Ivy says first, grabbing her water glass and taking a big swig. "Looks like tonight was a huge success despite your father showing up."

I frown. Great, did she notice? Or did Bryn tell her? "Yeah, well thanks to the dependable Miss James, who took care of everything and made sure he didn't cause too much of a scene."

"Yes, well thank goodness. You can always count on Miss James. Right, Bryn?" Ivy casts her an unreadable glance, which Bryn returns silently.

The vibe is completely off though Archer seems oblivious to it. They'd been talking about me. And somehow, someway, I must've pissed Bryn off. But how? She'd been so sweet to me right before she went and took care of my dad. How could it all have fallen apart in that short amount of time? Could Dad have said something to her, and she's keeping it to herself?

Shit.

"Well, listen I'm going to wander around and see if there's anything else that needs to be done," I say, gripping the chair in front of me.

"Off to play the gracious host, huh?" Archer asks, slinging his arm around Ivy's shoulders. She snuggles up closer to him and jealousy fills me, sharp and painful.

I wish I had the right to be as affectionate with Bryn. We're not even close to that comfort level yet. I touch her in front of Gage and Archer and they'll be all over me like white on rice, ready to call the entire bet off.

Not that I care about the million dollars, but damn it, it's the principle. I won that bet fair and square. I want to collect from them and rub it in their faces.

I feel like an immature asshole, but I want to win.

"Gotta do what I must to ensure everyone's having a good time," I say with a smile, glancing at Bryn to find her watching me with those all-seeing, sky-blue eyes.

"Do you need my help?" she asks.

"No, relax. Sit and enjoy the party. You dealt with enough already." I'm trying to communicate with her how much I appreciate her taking care of my dad. That couldn't have been easy. The old man is a grumpy asshole with a mouth that never, ever stops.

"Okay. As long as you're sure." She smiles but it doesn't quite reach her eyes. She looks so beautiful and so incredibly fragile sitting there next to the pregnant Ivy, who's glowing with vitality. Compared to her, Bryn's natural light from the last week is dimmed. She doesn't need the beige tonight. Even in magenta she looks subdued.

And I hate that. Knowing I'm the cause of it all.

"Could I talk to you for a moment though?" I suddenly ask. "Privately?" I need to make sure she's all right.

"Sure." She shrugs those beautiful, bared shoulders and stands, going round the table so she's next to me. I lead her away to another table at the far end of the courtyard, ignoring Archer since I can feel him watching me. Just waiting for me to slip up and somehow touch Bryn inappropriately in front of him.

Jackass.

"What's going on?" she asks when we stop to talk.

"Did my father say something to you? Did he offend you or try to put his hands on you?" I ask, cutting right to the point.

She sighs, hangs her head. "He said a few things. Nothing that I haven't heard before."

What the hell does she mean by that? "What are you talking about?"

Bryn lifts her head so her gaze meets mine once more. "He asked if the two of us were—sleeping together yet, though he phrased it a little more crudely."

I inwardly groan. "What did you tell him?"

"I told him we weren't, of course, which is the truth." She stresses the last word. "He didn't believe me."

"What a bastard," I mutter, running my hand through my hair in pure frustration. "How did you get him to leave?"

"Well, he wouldn't stop with the crude remarks and insults so I finally dragged him to his feet and hauled him out of here. Turned him over to the guys working valet, and they got him to his car," she explains matter-of-factly.

While I wish I could've been there by her side to defend her, I'm also proud of the fact that she handled herself so calmly. "You're amazing," I say softly, wishing I could touch her. But I can still feel Archer's eyes on me so there's no way I'm going to do it.

"I did what you asked. Don't make it out to be more than it was." She offers me a wan smile. "Is that all you wanted to ask me?"

"Bryn." Unable to help myself, I reach out and touch her arm lightly. Screw it. I don't care what Archer thinks. "Are you okay? You seem upset."

"Nothing like a little dose of reality to bring me back and remind me of what I really am." The smile turns brittle, and she inclines her head toward the rest of the partygoers circling in the courtyard. "You need to go talk to everyone else and make them all happy that they got a chance to speak to the owner of the new and rather impressive DeLuca Winery, don't you think?"

I let my hand drop. "Can I see you? Later tonight?"

She slowly shakes her head. "I don't think that's a good idea, Mr. DeLuca."

And with those last words, she walks away, leaving me in the dust.

Chapter Nine

Bryn

THE PHONE HAS been ringing constantly since I got into work this morning, but I blame that on the aftermath of the party. Everyone's looking for Matt, including me. Though I shouldn't. I'm not sure if I'm quite ready to face him yet.

I stayed home the entire weekend, not daring to go out, barely glancing at my phone. I ignored the calls and texts from Ivy and Marina, ignored the single text from Matt too. It wasn't work related so I figured I was safe. The text had come Saturday afternoon, asking if I'd survived the night okay, and I didn't bother answering.

How could I tell him the night had been a revelation? That I realized exactly who I am and what people saw when they looked at me? Well, specifically what men see, minus the bland outfits and boring hair.

That hurt, though deep down inside, I knew it. That's why I hid, pretending to be something I'm not.

Avoiding Ivy and Marina was tough because I would've loved to confide in them but what if my confession turned them against me? All the old worries and insecurities swamped me these last few days. It's hard to shake those old habits when they'd been such a part of my life for so long. Men don't respect me, they never have. I didn't have many friends growing up, and I definitely haven't had any since I've come to California.

I'm scared if I tell Ivy and Marina my fears, what happened between Matt and me, what his dad said about me, they'd see me differently. Dumb, I know since they're the ones who convinced me to go after Matt in the first place, but I can't help it. I'm afraid they'll know what I really am versus what I present. A silly dumb girl who is only thought of for her sexuality, not her brains or her skills.

And I don't know if I could face them, seeing the judgment in their eyes.

Besides, I know they kept reaching out to me because they only wanted to gossip about Friday night's party or analyze what happened between Matt and me. I'd rather not think about it at all. The more I do, the more upset I become, especially when the things his dad said to me come into play.

I bet you chase her around your desk all the damn time, trying to get your hands on that ass. I know I would.

Spending the majority of the weekend in bed watching bad TV and eating junk food didn't do anything to help my mood either. By the time I got my act together and prepared to go into work, I had bags under my eyes, my skin was kind of pale, I felt five pounds heavier, and I had a zit on my chin.

Great.

I showed up right on time though, not wanting to disappoint anyone—specifically Matt. Not wearing any beige or my severe hairstyle either, deciding to give in and go with what's natural for me, not the phony front I've put up since I've arrived here. Clad in the dress I wore last Monday, with the black background and blue and green flower and bird pattern, I leave my hair loose and hanging down my back.

I'm tired of the facade. Of being something I'm not. If I had my slightly trampy clothes from my time in Hollywood or even my wardrobe from Cactus, I'd be wearing them. Today. Right now.

But I don't have any of those clothes anymore. I burned most of them. It had felt like a cleansing of sorts, one I'd needed to start fresh.

Now I wish I had them. Just to remind me of my roots and who I really am. That reminder would fuel me and keep me strong for what I'm about to do today. Something I need to do.

I need to quit.

But Matt showed up late which made me antsy. He came in just past nine with a harried expression on his face, rushing into the room with the determination of a man on a mission. He'd dressed casually, jeans and a polo shirt that fit him to perfection.

My mouth literally waters when I see him now.

But what else is new?

"Had a meeting with the Napa Valley Vintners this morning," he says, stopping just in front of my desk. His mind is going a mile a minute, I can tell. "I need you to look into flights to New York City in a few weeks. We're going to attend the Savor Wine Guild annual convention. Had no idea it was going down, so I need to make arrangements quick."

I grab a pen and start jotting down notes. "What are the dates?"

"We'd have to leave two weeks from today," he says, whipping out his phone and scrolling through his emails.

My pen stills on the notepad, and I pause for a moment, his words slowly sinking into my dense brain. I glance up to find him watching me carefully. Almost too carefully. "Did you say we?"

"I want you to go with me, Bryn. I'll need your help. It's only for a few days but it's a busy few days. I'll want your input, and you'll have to keep me on task," he explains.

He wants me to go with him, alone, to New York City. I must be hearing things.

"Are you serious?"

"Serious as a heart attack." His expression is dead serious too. "You're my assistant right? I can't do this alone, Bryn. There's going to be a two-day forum with business discussions, workshops, and extensive, in-depth wine tastings. I can't be everywhere at once, so I need you to take on some of the workshops and talks or whatever, take notes and get back to me."

"Okay." I take a few more notes then turn to my computer and start searching for flights. "Are you sure you want to bring me though? I mean, really? Won't it be just an extra expense, my flight and hotel room, food and everything else that comes with traveling?"

"I need as many write-offs as I can get," he says dismissively. "And I can afford to bring you, Bryn. That's not an issue so don't worry about it."

All my plans of giving my notice to Matt fly right out the window at his rapid-fire requests. There's no way I can leave now. He needs me, as ridiculous as it sounds. Despite all the trouble I will no doubt bring him and the expectations he'll have, I need to be there for him.

I can do this. I'll work for the next two weeks, take the trip to New York, run around this convention with him for a few days, come home, and then I'll give my notice. That ought to give me enough time to find a job in Cactus, not that it should be too difficult.

I'd called my grandma last night, asking if I could go back and live with her in Cactus. She'd agreed readily, her booming voice coming at me over the phone, loud and reminding me why I left my hometown in the first place.

"Of course, you can come live with me, girl. I know Wanda down at the Soap-n-Snip needs a new phone girl. Maybe you could get your cosmetics license and make that career happen. It's a good one, you know. Why, that sweet little Becky who's only two years older than you has made herself quite the career working there."

Then she'd launched into a twenty-minute gossip session full of what's been happening in Cactus the last few years. By the time she finished, I knew everything. All of it.

Some stuff I found interesting. Other stuff I could care less about. Typical Cactus talk, all of it.

And soon I'll be back, right in the midst of it all. Working at the Soap-n-Snip, answering the phone, sweeping up hair and generally miserable with life.

At least I'll be in my element, back in my hometown. Where I can literally let down my hair, be free and be me.

I don't feel like I can be me anywhere else, not even here.

Especially not here.

"I'll find some flights and show you the options," I say, my voice crisp as I go into efficient mode.

"Great. Go to the Savor website and register us too. We'll probably have to pay for late registration, but I don't care. I can't miss this. The people at the Vintners said I must attend this event. We'll find out the latest trends, see both the business and the creative side of winemaking; it's going to be pretty awesome." He smiles, and I smile back unable to stop myself.

He's just so excited, so pumped to do this. I want to be excited for him. Even though I plan on disappointing him completely within the next month.

Matt

"You sly dog." Gage shakes his head just before he takes a bite of his cheeseburger. We're at a restaurant in downtown St. Helena, one that makes the best burgers and sandwiches and doesn't have a vegetarian or gluten-free option in sight. This is why the place is filled with mostly men. We've grown weary of the massive health movement that's taken over our area so easily.

"What are you talking about?" I ask, my voice neutral.

"You know. Taking the assistant to New York City where none of us can keep tabs on the two of you. Where you're free to walk around and hold hands, kiss her on the street, and fuck her all night in a hotel room. Smart move, man. Smart. Move." Gage laughs.

I ignore him, digging into my hamburger with gusto. I'm freaking starving, I've been so busy with work for the last three days: hardly taking a break, skipping lunches, staying late. Gage had been giving me endless shit, calling me the last two days saying he wanted to meet for lunch. Finally, after harassing me all morning with nonstop texts, I gave in, telling Bryn I'd be back in an hour and that if I didn't show up at the office by one-thirty, she needed to buzz me and get my ass back there.

When I'm with either Archer or Gage, we usually start talking about all sorts of crap and lose track of time, especially if there are beers involved.

Today, there aren't. I made sure of that.

"Does Archer know you're taking her to New York? I assume he does. I only found out because Marina told me after she spoke with Bryn yesterday. Like you'd ever tell us." Gage laughs some more. "I guarantee at the end of the forty-five days I'm going to find a way out of making this payment to you. Watch me. Why should we pay you when you're off fucking your assistant?"

"You have a dirty mind," I mutter, grabbing a fry and dipping it in catsup before I point it at him. "Not everything is about fucking, you know. How does Marina put up with your ass day in and day out?"

"Marina loves my ass. And she especially loves my dirty mind." He waggles his brows at me like a pervert. "And listen to you, the former king of groupies, chastising me like a prude. You sure as hell need to get laid and quick so we can cancel this entire bet once and for all. I'm tired of dealing with your insufferable ass."

"Yeah, yeah. Fuck off," I mutter, shaking my head, concentrating on my lunch. "You're the one who wanted to have lunch with me in the first place." He has a point. I'm grumpy as hell because I want Bryn, and she's turned off the signal completely. It's like she barely realizes I exist.

I know why though. It's because of my father. It's because of that kiss. I regret her having to deal with my dad and the things he said to her. I wish I could've protected her from that.

But the kiss? I don't regret that at all.

"I asked you to lunch so I could find out where your head is at." He takes a drink from his soda. "So tell me. Did you plan this so-called business trip on purpose to get her in your hotel room or what?"

"Not even," I scoff, munching on another fry. "We're attending a conference—and not some phony one either, which I'm sure you'll accuse me of. I won't even have time to think about doing anything else except going from workshop to workshop, attend wine tastings and the like.

It's all about the business, my friend. Something you've forgotten since you're too enraptured with your new girlfriend."

"Says the man taking his obsession with him to New York City so he can do *business*." Gage rolls his eyes. "Give me a break, man. We know exactly why you're taking Bryn with you. To get in her panties."

Thinking about Bryn in her panties just about gives me a coronary. So many lost opportunities we've had in such a short amount of time. Now she acts like she couldn't give two shits about me.

I hate it. And it's all my fault so I have no one to blame but myself.

"Definitely not," I say firmly. "I think she's over me."

"Ha!" Gage points at me, his gaze bright and full of triumph. "You admit it; you two *are* interested in each other."

"Yeah well, if she was interested in me, she's definitely not now. She's back to the efficient, no-nonsense Miss James."

"I bet she sure is hot though, when she's the efficient, no-nonsense Miss James," Gage says with a shit-eating grin.

Jealousy flaring, I throw a fry at him aiming for his face, but he dodges it just in time. "Shut up, dickhead. You're acting like a child." What the hell, I feel like lately we've reverted to college talk—when we were young and dumb and talked crudely to and about everyone, especially each other.

"Who's the child here, throwing food and calling me

a dickhead?" Gage shakes his head. "I don't know if any of us are going to survive these new terms. The longer you go without getting some, the grumpier you become. I bet your Miss James lost interest because you've become such a tyrant."

That can't be the reason. Can it? I doubt it. I think it has something to do with Dad. I have no idea what he said to her; she's not talking and neither is he. I called him up a few days ago and flat out accused him of saying something shitty to Bryn but he didn't give an inch.

Leaving me to conclude that he's guilty as hell.

"The DeLuca Winery is all anyone's talking about around town," Gage says, thankfully changing the subject. "Your reopening was a huge hit."

"Yeah, it went pretty well, didn't it?" I'm trying to downplay it more for my own sake than anything else. There are still some deals and transactions in the works—trying to get some regional markets to carry the DeLuca brand, pushing out and growing our distribution list. More publicity opportunities too, ones that I'm hopeful will come to fruition and take DeLuca wine to a national level.

Going to Savor will get the DeLuca brand out there even more. I've realized quick, especially after meeting with the local Vintners group, that I need to be constantly pushing the name, constantly talking to people in the industry. Creating a good wine is key, but networking is a necessity to selling good wine. Growing, learning, taking it all in—especially at conferences where I meet others in the business, so I can bring it back to DeLuca and apply everything I've learned—is important.

Do I really need to take Bryn with me to Savor? Probably not. I would've been exhausted running around that conference for two days, and missed a few talks or workshops I wanted to check out, but I could've done it all on my own. It's just so much more fun having her with me. And easier, of course, since she's beyond capable and will keep me on schedule.

Spending time with her on a plane, in the city, at a hotel. It's all ripe with possibilities.

If the woman I'm interested in actually acted interested in me, that is.

Chapter Ten

Bryn

Two weeks later, New York City

I SIT ON my cushy king-size bed with my laptop, glancing over my hand-scribbled notes taken from the endless amount of workshops I went to all day. I have never,
in all my life, stayed in a hotel like the W New York at
Times Square. Of course, the biggest city I've ever been
to before was Los Angeles and that's just a sprawling
metropolis with crowded freeways and shopping malls
everywhere.

New York City has a completely different vibe. All the
buildings are so tall, the sidewalks packed, and everything is open so late. I've never seen anything like it. In
my hometown, the sidewalks rolled up and shops closed
around eight o'clock, nine on Saturdays.

We arrived last night, and Matt had wanted a slice of

pizza at one in the morning. We'd promptly gone out and found a place open—not only open but packed.

It thrilled my small-town-bumpkin-self right down to my toes.

While I attended workshops today, Matt went to a discussion symposium, a special wine tasting, and currently he's at a keynote dinner. He tried to get me to go with him, but I declined, saying I'd rather call for room service and type up the notes I knew I'd have.

He'd reluctantly agreed, telling me I could order whatever I wanted from room service since he was paying for it.

It's funny, considering how hard I've seen him work and how many hours he's put in at the winery, a lot of the time I forget Matt's wealthy. As in billionaire-wealthy. The guy is loaded, thanks to both his father and Matt earning a bundle from his baseball contract and various endorsements.

And those are just the most recent ones.

It wasn't until we stepped on the plane and sat in first class that I saw how the other half lives. Talk about star treatment. I've flown once in my life and that was when I went to California—on a shitty little crowded plane that made me pay for a soda, for the love of God. I declined, sitting in my cramped little seat between two large, sweaty businessmen who leered at me the entire flight.

I hated it.

But flying first class in the wide comfy seats, being served constantly, and sitting next to Matt? I felt like I'd died and gone to heaven.

That was until I saw the hotel. Oh, my word, it was the prettiest, most modern hotel I've ever seen in my life, not that I've stayed anywhere beyond a Motel 6. I made sure Matt had a two-room suite with a gorgeous city view and since my room was right next to his—which he'd asked for—I had the same.

I didn't even care that I wasn't outside amongst the hustle and bustle of Times Square. I was perfectly content sitting in my suite with the gorgeous white bed and shocking pink comforter. The sleek glass furniture and the blooming hot pink orchids everywhere. Me, the Cactus, Texas-supposed-slut, feels like a real life fairytale princess.

All thanks to Matt.

What sucks? I have to give my notice when we return. There's just no way I can continue working for him. I'm pretending to be this certain type of quiet, demure woman when I'm not. My real self is bound to pop out sooner or later, and I don't want to do that in front of Matt. He thinks I'm a good girl.

And I can't seem to let go of my old, bad girl insecurities.

It's bad enough we've kissed a few times. The last thing I want to do is hurt his reputation, so I try my best to avoid him, but it's near impossible. The tension between us is still there though we never talk about it. I see the way he stares at me when he thinks I'm not looking. I want to return that longing stare. Worse, I want to lock myself away in his office, plop myself on his desk right in front of him and beg him to kiss me.

I think he'd take me up on the offer. I know he would.

But then I'd become the slut everyone accuses me of being. Sleeping with my boss to get ahead—at least, that's what it would look like. Indulging in a heated affair with the man who signs my paychecks is not smart. Didn't I learn anything after my failed attempt at a minor affair with Brian Fairbanks?

Leaning against the fabric headboard, I stare out the window at the city lights that surround me. I hadn't thought of his actual name since I don't remember when. I prefer to think of him as this faceless, nonentity, otherwise known as my ex-boss. It's just so much easier that way, not thinking of his name.

Now it all comes back to me. Brian would flash that charming smile as he whipped his thin blond hair away from his eyes, his gaze always eating me up. He had this way of making me feel like I was special, despite the ridiculous way he talked to me about titties and ass and how much his palm itched to give me a spanking.

Yes, he said that. He said a whole lot more too, plenty of which I wish to banish from my brain forever.

When I told my grandma what happened with Brian— how it turned out he had a wife and kids—she'd read me the riot act. Chewed me out for what felt like hours, though it probably only equaled about fifteen minutes. Told me if I continued flirting with these men who were in positions of authority, I'd never get ahead unless I had sex with them. That was all they thought of when they looked at me.

A sexpot. She'd called her own granddaughter a

sexpot though now I suppose she said it to warn me. I always heard how I needed to make good choices.

So I tried. I tried and tried and tried and here I sit, in a hotel suite paid for by my boss, and I'm still contemplating how I can get him into my room, so I can have a chance with him at least once before I quit and go back home to Cactus.

Have I lost my mind? I worry so much how others will see me, yet I still want Matt. I can't help it. If people are going to call me a sexpot, a slut, or a tramp, I guess I can go ahead and give them a reason to, right?

Respect yourself. If you don't, no one else will either.

I need to remember that.

My cell phone buzzes and I glance at it to see a text from Matt.

You in your hotel room?

I sure am, typing up notes just for you, I answer.

No reply, and I stare at the screen of my phone, willing something to appear. When nothing happens, I toss it aside and start typing up my notes again, my eyelids growing heavier with the menial task.

It was bad enough I had to sit through those sessions. Now I'm reliving them by rewriting the notes, reminding me exactly how boring they'd been.

Well, boring to me. Matt would probably find it fascinating since he's in the business but definitely not me.

My phone dings again, and I grab it.

You should meet me at the Blue Fin Restaurant downstairs in thirty minutes.

Why?

I chew on my fingernail, waiting for his answer. I already had room service for dinner, ordering a delicious pasta dish with shrimp and a salad on the side the moment I got back to the hotel. I'm not even hungry.

I want to take you out to dinner.

The Blue Fin is a gorgeous restaurant in the hotel; I keep peeking in there when I walk by. I'm dying to check it out but not like this.

Staring at my phone's screen, I contemplate how I should answer. The conference is over for the night. We have one more day tomorrow and then it's over. Dinner tonight isn't official business.

It feels personal. Like a date.

I already ate. Didn't you eat too?

Have dessert then. And the meal they gave us at the keynote was crap. I'm still hungry.

A little sigh escapes me, and I stare out the window again, drinking in the beautiful city view. I should decline. I should stay in my pretty hotel room and type up my messy notes and fall asleep in my deliciously soft bed. A good girl would do that. She wouldn't be tempted to do something bad, like go out on a dinner date with her boss.

But I never said I was a good girl.

I want to spend time with Matt. I want to go out to dinner with him and stare at his handsome face from across the table. I want to hear him tell me a story, and then I want to tell him a story and make him laugh. I want him to reach across the table and grab my hand, entwining our fingers.

I want it all, and I want it with Matt.

Grabbing my phone, my fingers hover over the keys for a millisecond before I start typing.

You said thirty minutes?

Yep, he replies. *We on?*

A smile curves my lips as I answer him.

We are definitely on.

Matt

I'M EXHAUSTED. THE jet lag, the running from one session to the next at the conference, the information coming at me from all sides, it's all depleting my energy. I should've just gone to my room, ordered room service and collapsed into a deep, dreamless sleep.

But none of that matters because here I am, waiting for Bryn at the entrance to the Blue Fin, eagerness at seeing her making my stomach jump like a pond full of hyperactive fish. I've hardly seen her since we arrived in New York City. We've been on separate schedules, meeting up in odd spots, like in the corridor of the event center earlier this afternoon. I'd been rushing by, but I called her name when I noticed her exiting a room.

She'd waved, looking adorable in dark-rinse jeans that fit her sexy legs perfectly, a secretive smile curling those sensual lips.

My cock had literally twitched at seeing her, even for such a fleeting second.

"Hi. Hope I didn't keep you waiting."

I turn at the first sound of her sultry voice, smiling

when I see Bryn standing before me. She'd changed and is now wearing a sleek, simple long-sleeved black dress that covered pretty much every available inch of her save her face, hands, calves and feet. Yet somehow she still manages to be sensual as hell, what with the way the fabric clings lovingly to her body.

"Miss James. I must say you're looking extra beautiful this evening."

Her cheeks color, turning a beautiful shade of pink as she clutches her hands in front of her. "Thank you," she murmurs, her gaze meeting mine for the briefest second before she lets it drop. "You look good too."

I'm still in the black trousers I've worn all day but changed into a white button-down shirt right after I texted her, wanting to dress up a little bit since I figured the Blue Fin had something of a dress code. I'd planned on going to dinner alone. Well, I told myself that. "Thank you. Ready to be seated?"

When she nods, I lead her to the front desk, requesting a table for two. The hostess grabs two menus and leads us up the floating stainless steel staircase to a semi-private alcove, filled with quiet booths that line the wall and overlook the bright lights of Times Square. A small jazz quartet plays along the opposite wall—soothing, soft music that adds to the hushed atmosphere.

"You're not hungry?" I ask after the hostess leaves us, flipping open the menu immediately. "I'm starved. Conference chicken and dry rice pilaf doesn't do much for my appetite."

She laughs, the sweet sound washing over me, making me yearn. For her. "Sounds awful."

"It was." I glance over the entrees, my stomach grumbling at some of the offerings, especially the blue cheese-encrusted filet mignon. "I know what I'm having," I say, shutting the menu.

"So do I," she says, closing hers as well, her sparkling gaze meeting mine. She looks extra pretty in the candlelight, and I can smell her. That intoxicating scent of hers that drives me wild. I don't know if I can withstand it much longer.

"You getting dessert?"

"I think so. I filled up on a pasta dish from room service earlier. It was delicious." She smiles, a mysterious little curve of her lips that makes me want to discover all of her secrets. She has lots of them. I don't know much about her, and I wish I did. Seeing her like this, spending time with her, fills me with greed.

I want more. More of Bryn.

"That's what I should've done rather than listening to that guest speaker. He was boring." I take a sip of my ice water, hoping it'll cool my suddenly heated skin. Just watching her, how the candle flickering on our table casts her face in a golden glow, I'm mesmerized by how beautiful she is, how at ease she seems to be with me tonight. This is a first. We haven't felt this comfortable with each other in weeks.

"We should've ditched the conference altogether today and explored the city," Bryn suggests. "I know we're here to work, but I've never been to New York City before."

"It's kind of crazy, isn't it?"

She nods. "I feel like a total hick coming here. Like I want to stop in the middle of the sidewalk and just stare at everything. All the people, the noise, the lights, the smells—I've truly never seen anything like it. Cactus has nothing on this place."

I like it when she talks about her past, which isn't often enough for my liking. It offers a glimpse into her world that I don't get to see. She's a private person, and I can't blame her but I'm still curious.

The waiter approaches and we order drinks—water for Bryn and a beer for me—plus a crab cake appetizer that I offer to share but she passes on it.

"I don't really do seafood," she says, wrinkling her nose.

Damn, she's cute. I notice when she gets tired or feels comfortable, the southern accent makes a faint appearance.

"Really? I love it."

"We don't get much seafood in Cactus if you know what I mean. It's terribly dry and flat and not an ocean in sight."

We grew up in completely different worlds. I'd spent my entire life in the Bay Area, bouncing around as my dad moved us from place to place, but never really straying. Growing up by the ocean in such a huge city, I never realized what an effect it had on me. How it made me view the world. For Bryn, growing up in such a small town in the middle of nowhere had profound effects on her too. "What made you leave your hometown?"

"There was nothing there for me." Her expression shutters, and I wonder why. It always feels like there's more behind her reasoning, and she's just not telling me. "It's a small town that's going nowhere. I would've gone nowhere." She tears her gaze from mine, staring off into space. "But sometimes if you have no other choice, you have to settle for nowhere, you know?"

No, I didn't know, but I'd never been one to settle. If there was something I wanted, I went after it until it was mine. I liked a challenge. "Settling for nowhere sounds like a last resort."

"What if you've tried all the resorts and none of them worked out?" she asked, her voice dropping to a low murmur as her gaze meets mine once again, her eyes wide, her expression . . . forlorn.

I immediately want to comfort her. Wrap her in my arms and reassure her everything's going to be all right. I don't even know what I'd be referring to, but I don't care. She brings out a protectiveness in me I didn't even realize I had.

"What are you talking about Bryn?" There's definitely more going on here than what she's saying, and I want to know what it is.

"I left home because I had a bad experience at a job." A funny little smile crosses her lips, and I wonder what sort of bad experience she's talking about. "Then I moved to Los Angeles because I decided to become a model. I'm tall, I have a decent face, and I decided I was going to use my natural assets to get a job. But that was a disaster."

I can only imagine. I've heard plenty of firsthand stories of how Hollywood chews up these pretty, naive girls and spits them out.

Bryn was gorgeous enough that I wouldn't doubt she had a lot of interest. Probably all of it overtly sexual though, since so many of the sleazy photographers and directors that line the Hollywood streets won't do anything for a girl unless she sleeps with them first.

"So the job at the winery was a last ditch effort before I had to go back home for good. I found the job on Craigslist. I loaded up my old Saturn with my few boxes of stuff and drove north to the land of new opportunities. Only to discover the winery was hanging by a thread and eventually we weren't even getting paid properly. Until you walked in and saved us all."

The waiter chooses this moment to show up with our drinks and my appetizer, interrupting Bryn's story. I wait impatiently as he places everything in front of us and takes our dinner orders—well my dinner order since Bryn chose salted caramel cake for her dessert. He even tries to make conversation, and I finally glare at him until he gets the hint and takes off.

"Matt, that was kind of rude," Bryn chastises the moment the waiter's gone. "He was just trying to do his job and be nice."

"He interrupted you." I grab my silverware and place my napkin in my lap before I dig into the crab cake. It smells amazing, the sauce that comes with it is delicious and my starving stomach is applauding my choice even as I begin eating. "Go on," I prompt her after I swallow.

"I was pretty much done. You were my savior and now

here we sit, in New York City. You showing the country bumpkin how the big city folk live." She props her elbow on the edge of the table and rests her chin on her fist. "You've taught me a lot in a short amount of time, Matt, and for that I'm eternally grateful."

She's speaking with a finality that makes me uneasy. "I'll show you more if you let me," I say, going with the double meaning behind my words. Why pretend any longer? I'm sick of it. I don't know if she is too, considering she's been running pretty hot and cold lately, but I am one who goes after something—or someone—once I realize I want it.

And I want her. Bryn. I'm tired of fighting my attraction for her.

Her arm drops from the table as she leans back in her chair. "What do you mean by that?"

I shrug. "Take from it whatever you want."

She studies me for a long, quiet moment, her gaze roving over my face before she finally reaches for her water glass and drains half of it. "I won't sleep with you, Matt," she says after she sets the glass on the table.

I'm shocked yet pleased at her boldness. "What I'm suggesting won't involve any sleeping, Bryn."

Her lips part as her eyes widen the slightest bit. "We shouldn't."

"Why not?"

"I work for you."

"I know. That little fact does make my attraction for you rather—awkward." There. I said it. And I'm not taking it back either.

"I've tried resisting you." She drops her head, studies her lap, and I want to reach for her. Pull her into my arms and offer her reassurance, let her know she's not alone in this confusing sea of emotions and wants and needs.

I'm right there with her, drowning in the swirling sea, hoping she'll be the one who finally throws me an anchor and tows me in.

"I've tried resisting you too," I confess in a low murmur. "Clearly it's not working since I still want you."

"Is it a case of wanting what you can't have?" Her head is still bent, her voice so soft I can hardly hear it.

My appetite has fled. I set my fork on the edge of the plate and push it away. All I can think about, all I can want is this woman sitting across from me. "No. It's a case of wanting what I've had a taste of, and needing more of it. More of you."

She slowly lifts her head, her gaze meeting mine. "I got in trouble for doing this before."

I frown, confused by her change of subject. "For doing what?"

"Fooling around with my boss. I was nineteen. It was my first real job. My boss flirted with me and really turned on the charm until he finally wore me down, and I fell under his spell." She pauses, licking her lips. "He literally chased me around his desk all the time. It turned into this . . . game, and I actually liked the chase. Finally I let him catch me."

"What happened?" Dread fills me. I don't think I want to hear her answer.

"I . . . let him kiss me. A lot. And . . . and more. We

had sex, right there in his office. He made all of these promises to me, and I believed him. Oh, how I believed him. I thought I'd met the perfect man for me. Older, experienced, and sophisticated. I thought he would take me out and show me the world." She makes this funny little face, rolling her eyes, and smirking like she can't believe how silly she was. "Then I found out he was married and had a child. His wife called me and yelled at me. Told me she found text messages he'd sent me, and I couldn't believe he kept them on his phone. She called me a whore and a slut and a home wrecker."

"You were young," I say in her defense. "And he tricked you."

"I was dumb. And a home wrecker just like she said. How could I not know he was married? Cactus is a tiny town. I should've known." She presses her lips together, looking ready to cry.

I reach across the table and grab her arm, lifting it up so I can interlace our fingers, giving her hand a squeeze. "Hey, stop. Don't beat yourself up. You didn't know."

"I was an idiot," she sniffs.

"No you weren't." Her boss was a jackass of the worst kind. Taking advantage of a young, naive girl. Getting her to fall for him all while he was married.

"I had sex with my married boss."

"I'm not that guy. And I'm definitely not married." I reach for her with my other hand, slipping my fingers beneath her chin and lifting her face up. "And I don't have any kids either. You can kiss this boss all you want."'

She smiles in spite of it all, a beautiful, bright, and

toothy smile unlike any I think I've ever seen her display. "I like you, Matthew DeLuca. A lot."

"Enough to kiss me again?" I ask, my heart starting to pick up speed.

"We shouldn't."

"There are lots of things we shouldn't do." Leaning in, I hover just above her lips, feel her breath feathering across my own. "Sometimes we just have to do it anyway."

Chapter Eleven

Bryn

HE KISSES ME after he says that. His mouth touches mine gently before he lifts away from me to flash a quick smile. He dips down and kisses me again, for real this time, with heat and tongue and little moans and rough groans. I lose myself in his taste, in the way he squeezes my fingers in his, how his fingers hold my chin and softly caress my skin.

Right here in a booth in the middle of a restaurant in the middle of Times Square, Matt kisses me like he means it. After he hears bits and pieces of my sordid story, it's like it didn't even affect him. Oh, he showed sympathy in all the right places—shock and horror and disgust—but never at me. It was like he understood what happened.

And kissed me anyway.

Someone clears their throat, and I spring away from Matt to find the waiter standing before our table, holding a tray with our plates on it and a smug smile on his face. Matt scoots away from me reluctantly, letting go of my hand as the waiter scoops up his appetizer, which he'd hardly eaten.

The salted caramel cake is set before me, and my mouth waters at the sight. It's white cake with caramel sauce and berries sprinkled on top, the sticky sweet smell making me breathe deep, a little smile on my face. I glance over in Matt's direction to see he's watching me, his expression hungry, his massive steak sitting in front of him forgotten as he continues to watch me.

"Enjoy your meal," the waiter says before he vacates, and I can't help but think yes, indeed we're going to enjoy our meal.

But what I'm really looking forward to is what we're going to do *after* the meal.

I know Matt feels the same way.

"HAVE YOU SEEN my room?" Matt asks the moment he pulls me into the empty elevator, my hand clasped in his.

I slowly shake my head, loving how close I'm standing next to him. I can see the dark stubble dotting his cheeks, the scar just on the underside of his chin. He glances down at me, smudges of darkness just below his eyes show that he hasn't been sleeping very well. Considering how busy he's been lately, this doesn't surprise me.

"I'm pretty sure we have identical rooms," I say, hoping he realizes I'm teasing.

"Ah, mine is better. I can almost guarantee it." He

squeezes my hand and tugs me close, so I'm standing in front of him, my back to his front. Releasing his grip on my hand, he settles his big, warm palms on my shoulders and starts rubbing. "You're tense."

I don't have the heart to tell him he's the one making me tense. All the sexual tension that's swirled between us for the last few weeks and months—it's overwhelmed me.

The elevator doors slide open and Matt gives me a push so I exit with him right behind me. We go to his room, and I wait with jumpy anticipation as he slides the keycard into the slot, the little light above the handle turning green. He opens the door, and I trail behind him inside, a shocked gasp escaping me when he turns and presses me against the door.

His hands rest at my waist as he pins me in place, his head dipping toward mine. Our mouths meet. I exhale against his lips, feel him smile before he takes the kiss deeper and then there's no time for breathing or thinking or saying a word.

All I can do is savor. Savor the sensation of his mouth on mine, his fingers digging into the fabric of my dress, my skin. The cool metal of the door is shocking against my backside, paired with the pure heat radiating from Matt's big body as he steps in so close to me, he's all I can see and feel and smell. His tongue thrusts, his hands tug at the fabric of my dress, lifting, lifting, until I feel cool air on my thighs and realize he's pulling my skirt up.

I tear my lips from his, desperate for us to slow down. My brain needs to catch up with my body before I do something really crazy and stupid. "I thought you were going to show me your room."

Matt drifts his mouth down the length of my neck, covering it in hot, wet little kisses. I grow slick between my legs with just his mouth pressed against my neck, and I clutch at him for fear I might fall. "I thought you said your room is exactly like mine," he whispers against my skin.

"I'd still like to see it." I press at his shoulders, trying to get him to back off just a little without having to say it. I need the space. I like having him in *my* space but still . . .

I'm not real good at this sort of thing. As in, I don't have a lot of experience. Especially with a man surely as experienced as Matthew DeLuca—in his previous life as a ballplayer, he must've had beautiful women constantly throwing themselves at him.

He lifts his head, his dark gaze meeting mine, and then he drops his hands from my waist as he steps away. "Come on, then. I'll show you around."

I pull my skirt back into place as I follow him deeper inside the room, my legs still shaking from the potency of his kiss, his touch. The effect he has on me is so powerful, so unbelievably overwhelming, I'm not sure what to think, or how to think.

"So? Is it just like yours?" he asks as we approach the window that overlooks the city.

I glance around, notice the orchids, the bright pink throw across the foot of his bed, the sleek, glass furniture. "Definitely. It's almost identical."

"You must have a really great boss then," he says, a

smile playing at the corners of his mouth. God, he's sexy. "Putting you up in a fancy hotel like this."

"He's pretty great," I say, my voice soft. "He's smart, successful, extremely wealthy, but he never throws it around. In fact, I tend to forget he's so well off."

His smile fades and his expression goes serious. "Do you prefer that, Bryn? Does my—financial status intimidate you?"

I shrug, trying to push down my small-town-hick worries so they don't rise to the surface like they always try and do when I talk money and status and wealth. "A little bit," I admit.

It's something I never even realized before. Matt can have anything he wants. Can go out and buy whatever he wants, he has so much money. He's a billionaire for the love of God, yet I know he doesn't live in a giant mansion, I've never seen him drive an outrageously fancy car beyond his sensible—but gorgeous—Range Rover. He's not flashy, not outrageous, like I can only assume his father can be.

And I find that extremely attractive, how simply he lives. If he'd been such a blatant, wealthy man, like Archer Bancroft, who intimidates the shit out of me every time I'm around him, I don't think I would've been able to handle Matt.

But he's not like that at all. He's gentle and kind and sweet and hardworking and sexy as all get out.

"Don't let it." He comes to me and presses his mouth to mine in a lingering, drugging kiss. "You did forget to mention one thing about me though."

I frown up at him and give in to what I've wanted to do all night. I touch his face, span my fingers across his cheek, so I can feel the slightly rough prickle of his stubble against my palm. "What?"

"My charismatic good looks." He grins, and I laugh, but he muffles my laughter in seconds with his mouth, kissing me so deliciously deep my head is spinning, my legs grow weak and I slump against him, lost in his taste and the way his arms grip me around my waist.

I pull out of his embrace without a word, and he lets me. I go to the window, desperate to gather my racing thoughts while I stare at the city spread out before me. Pressing my fingers against the cool glass, I gaze down and watch the bright lights of Times Square flash, the seemingly millions of people that fill the sidewalks, the cars, the streets.

"Your view is familiar," I tell him from over my shoulder, smiling when I feel him stop just behind me, just like he did when we were in the elevator. But this time he doesn't touch my shoulders.

He settles his big hands at my hips, giving them a firm squeeze before he lets them wander down across my backside. "Nervous?"

I close my eyes, losing myself in his assured touch, the way he squeezes and massages my skin. Everything inside me melts when he slowly tugs my skirt up, until the fabric is bunched just below my butt, my legs, my thighs completely exposed. "Yes," I admit on a whisper.

"Don't be. I'll go slow," he promises, and I believe him. "Christ, you've got the sexiest legs I've ever seen."

He grips my hips and pulls me toward him slightly, so I'm bent at the waist, my butt thrust out.

It's overtly sexual, the way he has me positioned. And when he steps closer, my backside brushing against the front of his jeans, I bite my lip to keep a moan from spilling out.

"Move closer to the window," he commands, and I do so keeping in position as best I can. His hands slip beneath the bunched fabric, touching my hips, and his fingers curl around the skimpy waistband of my panties. He pulls them down, over my butt, down my thighs and then I'm helping him, kicking them off while they get tangled around my shoes. I go to pull those off as well but his dark command stops me.

"Keep the shoes on."

Oh. My.

Matt

HER PANTIES ARE solid white lace, a scrap of fabric that probably barely covered her, not that I'll ever know now, since we tugged them off and they're now lying discarded on the floor nearby.

Not that I'm protesting.

She's a contradiction. Innocent yet sexy, with the face of an angel and a body made for sin. One minute she's shy and acts inexperienced, the next she's a laughing, sultry mistress who looks like she wants to devour me in one swallow.

I like it. I fucking love it and want to discover more

about her, everything that she holds within, everything that makes her who she is. But she holds out on me. She told me bits and pieces of her past earlier at dinner. She's a woman who's run from her problems. She acts like she might run from me.

But I won't let her. After tonight, she'll know who she belongs to.

Me.

I've waited for this moment for far too long to prolong it further, so I grip her by her hips and grind against her, let her feel my hard cock against her lush ass. She hangs her head down and moans, the agonized sound going straight to my dick and hell, I want to thrust in her now. Just fill her with my cock and know what it's like to finally be a part of her.

That's what I seek. That connection—the union of our bodies and minds and souls. I want it, I fucking need it, and I grasp hold of the ends of her thick, dark hair, pulling gently until she lifts up, turns her head so I can kiss her with everything I have inside of me.

She gasps against my mouth, her arm curving around my head, keeping me close as our tongues thrust against one another, our bodies doing the same. I want to take her just like this. I know it's not the most romantic position in the world, but at the moment, I'm not feeling very romantic.

I feel possessive. Like I want to mark her and let her know she's mine. I break our kiss, help her tear off her dress and then she's standing before me in a matching white lace bra, those sexy black heels and nothing else.

Damn, she's gorgeous. I can see her pink nipples, hard and thrusting against the innocent white lace, her breasts so full they threaten to spill out over her bra. "Take it off," I say gruffly, pointing at her chest.

She does so without hesitation, her hands going behind her to undo the clasp and then the bra is gone, fluttering to the floor to join her panties. She's standing before me completely naked save for the shoes while I'm still fully dressed.

Fuck me, that it. I'm done for.

The million dollar bet be damned. I could give a shit if Archer or Gage find out I've been with Bryn. What's done is done.

I have to have her.

Reaching behind me, I grab my wallet and flip it open, pulling out the single condom I keep nestled inside. I haven't been with a woman in months. I'm fucking afraid I'll come the moment I slide inside Bryn's body but I close my eyes, breathe deep to try and keep my libido in check.

But it's going to be so fucking hard.

"I want to fuck you right here," I whisper as I step into her space, her naked body pressed against the cool glass, my body pressed close to hers. "From behind, with you looking down at the view. Wondering if anyone can see us."

She releases a trembling breath. "A-all right."

"Does that bother you? Us having sex like this for the first time?" I kiss the top of her ear, the spot just behind it. Push her heavy hair aside so I can brush my mouth against her nape, along her shoulder. Her skin is soft, fragrant with the unique scent that drives me fucking wild, and I lean into her for a long, lingering moment, overwhelmed at what she does to me, how she makes me feel.

"No," she says softly as she circles her hips, her ass brushing against my denim-covered erection. "I-I think I like it."

I close my eyes, relieved that she's given her permission. I don't want to push, she's fragile, I can tell, and no way am I going to screw up tonight.

I grasp her face with one hand and she turns toward me, our mouths colliding, tongues sliding against each other. With my other hand I fumble with my belt buckle, desperate to get it undone so I can unsnap my jeans and pull my cock out. Roll the condom on and thrust inside her nice and slow, watching as I enter her body for the first time.

A full shiver moves through me and I break the kiss, trying to gain some control. "Brace your hands on the window," I tell her and she does, spreading her legs, and I step back checking out the view of her pretty pink depths.

Groaning, I touch her there, sliding two fingers between her legs. She's drenched, soaking wet, and I finish undoing my belt buckle, then tear open the button fly of my jeans. She's thrusting against my fingers, subtle lifts of her hips, and I brush against her clit, hear her gasp and moan.

My quest to get out of my jeans momentarily forgotten, I stroke her deeper, thrusting my fingers inside her velvety hot channel, driving us both crazy with lust. I want to get her off with my fingers, want to watch her fall apart by my hand, and I start whispering dirty words in her ear. How much I want to fuck her, how wet she is, how good she feels. She tilts her head back, her eyes closed, her mouth open as she pants frantic little breaths and then she's coming all over my fingers, her inner walls trembling, her entire body wracked with shudders.

I have to get inside her. Now.

Within seconds I have the condom on, and I slowly enter her still-trembling body, sliding deep, groaning as I fill her completely. She relaxes into me as I hold myself still, letting her get used to me being inside her, around her, holding her. Her back is covered in a light sheen of sweat, her fragrance even stronger as it fills my senses, and I slowly start to move.

In and out, my movements are shallow, teasing as I draw the moment out. Her hips start to move with my every thrust, and soon I'm increasing my pace, Bryn keeping up with me as she pushes back every time I push forward, taking me deep, deeper, until I can go no farther. I'm completely embedded in her.

I am hers. And she is mine.

"Harder," she gasps when I slow down, that familiar tingling sensation at the base of my spine telling me I'm about to come and it's going to be a big one.

"Baby, I go any harder, and I'm coming right now," I confess through clenched teeth.

"That's okay," she whispers, turning her head to glance at me over her shoulder. Her expression is one of wonder and pure, unadulterated pleasure. "Please, Matt."

She doesn't need to beg. I grip her hips and begin to

move within her in earnest. Again and again, harder and harder until I'm coming, her name falling from my lips as I erupt again and again, my orgasm strong as I go still above her, unable to move, only able to revel in the exquisite sensation of coming inside Bryn for the first time.

Chapter Twelve

Matt

I AM ON top of the fucking world. I fell asleep with Bryn in my arms, her naked body wrapped all around mine, her fragrant hair in my face. We woke up twice in the middle of the night, coming together easily, so easily, both times. The first was by my initiative, when I started kissing her down the length of her body, between her legs, until I had her writhing and coming apart beneath my lips and tongue.

She returned the favor, sucking me so deep inside her mouth I groaned loud enough to probably wake up the entire floor of the hotel. She made me come in an embarrassingly short amount of time.

The second time, she woke me up. It was her turn to rain kisses all over my body, driving me crazy with her lush, wet mouth. She finally grabbed a condom, slipped it on me and then rode me into oblivion, making herself come by grinding against my cock.

That had been hot. So hot I gripped her body and flipped her over so she was pinned beneath me and I drove myself inside her again and again, coming until I was a gasping, exhausted mess.

We collapsed in each other's arms, slept the rest of the night away until the alarm on my cell phone woke us up, reminding us of our sole purpose for being here.

The Savor conference.

We took a shower together before she slipped into a robe and snuck into her room, where she continued to get ready. We then took a taxi together to the conference since the weather was shit.

I held her hand the entire ride over, our fingers linked casually together, a representation of our relationship and how I was feeling. Usually that sort of shit scares me to death but not this time. Not with Bryn. I want her in my life. I don't care that she works for me. Hell, she can become my partner, helping me run the winery, making decisions—everything she already does.

I love the idea so much I know I'm going to mention it to her later tonight when we meet up again after the day's activities at the conference are over. She might balk and say she doesn't deserve the position, and that's one thing I've realized since I've started working with her: Bryn doesn't believe in herself very much.

She should though. She's talented and smart and keeps me on track like no one else. She offers thoughtful opinions and is always, always thinking ahead when it comes to the business. DeLuca Winery is always at the forefront of her thoughts and she's exactly what I need.

Bryn is all I need.

I move through the day like a giddy asshole in love, which is sort of how I feel. I can't concentrate, can't focus on what the speaker is saying at a very important, highly anticipated keynote I'm sitting in on. Instead I bounce my foot against the floor, thinking of last night. How Bryn felt in my arms. The taste of her nipples. The sounds she makes and what she looks like when she comes. That satisfied little smile that curled her lips this morning when I rolled her over and told her she should join me in the shower.

Yeah, I can't let any of that go. I don't want to let any of it go. I really think Bryn and I could make this happen.

First I need to confirm that she's interested in taking it further than a simple affair while we're out of town.

When I finally make it back to the hotel, I know she's already there since she texted me about an hour ago. I'm eager, ready to tell her my grand ideas about our personal and business future together, planned when I should've been listening to the state of the future of winemaking.

Ah well, fuck it. I'd rather think about Bryn.

But the moment I enter my hotel room I can sense the mood has changed. She's sitting on the edge of the bed—I gave her a key before we left earlier—her head bent as she scans through something on her phone. Her shoulders are slumped, her hair falling forward and shielding her face. There's something wrong.

I can feel it in the air.

"Hey." I say, letting the door shut softly behind me. "You all right?"

She lifts her head, her watery gaze meeting mine, and my heart lurches in my chest. She's been crying. Why? Over me?

God, I hope not.

"What's wrong?" I ask as I rush toward her, and she holds out her phone, averting her head so she doesn't have to look at me.

"Read this," she says, her voice rough with unshed tears.

I take the phone from her, see that she's brought up an article from a prominent gossip site. There's a hazy photo of Bryn and me at the window, her skirt bunched around her waist, white panties on brief display. You'd have to be an idiot not to realize what we're doing. I'm standing behind her, my hands resting on her hips.

The headline alone makes my heart drop into my toes:

Former Baseball Player Matt DeLuca Rounds the Bases With His Secretary!

"Shit," I say aloud as I sit heavily on the edge of the mattress right next to her, skimming the article. It goes on about Bryn and me, how she's worked for me since I took over the winery, and we've been having a heated affair for months. The unidentified source talks about our supposed affair and how it will be the eventual demise of my new business venture if I don't watch it.

The final nail in the coffin? The source goes on to say I'm just like my father, who's been embroiled with one scandal after another ever since the beginning of his career with the Oakland A's:

"Like father, like son, the apple doesn't fall far from the tree. Though at least the dad always seems to land on his feet. We'll see if his son can do the same."

"Who the fuck could've done this?" I ask grimly, thrusting the phone back toward her. I have my suspicions. I just don't want to say them out loud yet. "We need to figure out who's behind every word of this stupid, deceitful article."

Her head is still bent, like she can't stand to look at me. "It's not lies. It's the truth."

"It wasn't the truth until last night and that doesn't count," I tell her as I pull out my own phone to find a few text messages from Archer and Gage, both of them asking what the hell is going on with the article being blasted all over the place.

Oh and I have a voicemail from my father. Interesting.

I refuse to listen to it. Not now, in front of Bryn. I need to keep my emotions under control before I lose it completely.

I think he might have had a hand in this. The tone of the entire article makes me think he's behind it. That the article actually mentioned my father multiple times when he hasn't been in the spotlight in years makes me suspect him.

"Doesn't count?" She lifts her head, her angry eyes meeting mine. "Are you saying what happened between us last night doesn't count?"

"No. Of course not." I slowly shake my head, amazed

at all the emotion I see blazing in her gaze. "I think—shit, I think my dad could be behind this. God knows when he could've tried to first sell this article, probably right after the opening, when you so kindly pushed him out and sent him on his merry way."

"I didn't kindly push him out," she admits. "He said horrible things and basically accused me of being a slut and sleeping with his son. Oh, and when I grew sick of you, he said I could come and have sex with him any time I wanted. You know, because the two of you are so similar and all." She lets out an angry little sound that's a cross between a growl and a squeal. "The man is a pig."

Fuck. Tell me all about it. The worst part? He's my father. And supposedly I'm just like him.

"He said that to you?" I ask weakly, wincing when she stands to glare down at me, her expression one of pure fury.

"Yes! He made me feel like the cheap hussy everyone else seems to think I am. And look, we proved him right by having sex." She throws her arms up in the air. "I'm exactly what everybody says I am. A stupid whore who sleeps her way around, who just falls into bed with her boss because she's too dumb to know better."

I stand, grabbing hold of her shoulders and giving her a little shake. "No. Stop calling yourself such horrible names. You're nothing like that. We've been fighting this and trying to do the right thing for months, Bryn. Months. You didn't just fall into bed with your boss because you're too dumb to know better. I hope you came into my bed because you care for me as much as I care for you."

Bryn

I STARE INTO Matt's eyes, shocked by his words, by his easy defense of me. I ... I don't know what to say. I'm overwhelmed, upset, embarrassed. At least my name isn't in the article though, it doesn't need to be. There's the photo as proof it's me. Everyone at the winery will see the article and the picture, and I'll become a mockery. People in the community will hear the rumors and know I'm the one who's supposedly having a torrid affair with my boss.

It's the type of humiliation I've been trying to run from since Brian Fairbanks chased me around his office. I'd kept myself above it all, all these years. Running just ahead so that it never touched me.

But look at me now, neck deep in a huge scandal, and I have no one to blame but myself.

"Say something." Matt gives me another little shake, rattling me out of my thoughts. "I need to know if you're as invested in this as I am."

"Invested in what?" I ask, feeling like I'm in a daze.

"Invested in us," he says, his mouth grim, his eyes dark, fathomless. "Tell me. I need to hear you say it."

"I-I don't know how I feel, Matt," I say truthfully, horrified when I see the devastation cross his face.

God. I can't get this sort of thing right no matter how hard I try.

"So you don't want to be with me," he says, his voice dull as he releases his hold on me.

"I never said that." I watch as he turns his back on me

and runs his hand through his hair, an exasperated little sound escaping him.

My heart, my entire body aches to go to him. Offer him comfort and let him know we won't let this stumbling block break us. We can survive this.

But I don't know if that's the truth.

"I don't know what I want," I say when he doesn't speak. "Last night was . . . it was amazing. One of the best nights of my life, but after seeing this article today and the photo, I don't know what to think of it. Of us being together. Will we be dealing with this sort of thing for the rest of our relationship? Can we survive this type of scrutiny?" I'm scared not only of the media but of what others might think of us together. His friends, his peers in the industry. I don't want to bring him down.

I don't want to embarrass him.

He turns to face me, his expression full of confusion and anger and frustration. I feel terrible. I'm the one who's doing this to him, who's putting him through all this. "This is a fluke, Bryn. I'm pretty much out of the public eye and have been for over a year. No one cares that I have a winery in the Napa Valley, except for people in the freaking Napa Valley. Otherwise, I'm long forgotten. Some new young ballplayer has taken my place, and I'm fine with it. I've moved on. But my dad? He hates that I'm out of the public eye. Hates that he is too. He's fed the media stories about me for years."

"You really think he's behind this?" I ask incredulously. My grandma may drive me crazy and has heaped on plenty of helpings of tough love, but she would never blatantly sabotage me or spread such lies.

He grabs his phone, punches a button and holds it to his ear, his expression grim, eyes blazing with anger. He must be listening to his voicemail or something. I wait nervously, wrapping my arms around my middle, my mind racing.

What if the photographer took more pictures? What if they release more to the media over the next few days? God, what will that do to us?

"He left me a message asking if I'd seen the article, sounding like a smug asshole," Matt says, knocking me from my thoughts. "And hell yes, I do, especially after what you just told me. If he said those kind of things to you, then he could definitely be behind this. I mean, no one else would mention my dad and he just happens to appear in this stupid article. He's our unidentified source." He exhales loudly and pushes his fingers through his hair. "Wonder how much the asshole got paid for spreading these lies. I wonder who he got to follow us."

"Right. And who knows if any more pictures will show up? I will die if that happens, I swear. I can't live like this," I say, my voice soft yet steely while inside my nerves are in absolute chaos. "I can't do it, Matt."

"What are you talking about?" he asks, and I close my eyes, afraid to look at him, scared to see the sadness in his gaze.

"Having to deal with this sort of thing will wreck my self-esteem, and it's already pretty wrecked." I crack open my eyes to find him staring at me, shock written all over his handsome face. "I'll never be able to escape the shadow of being the home wrecker, the easy girl. The dumb slut who sleeps with her boss because she thinks that's what she's supposed to do."

"But that's not what we have, Bryn. Can't you see it? This has nothing to do with me being your boss and you being my assistant. What we have, what we shared last night, is about us being a man and a woman who are attracted to each other." He pauses, staring at me. "Right?"

I can only look at him, not sure what to say, how to defend my feelings. They are what they are, and I have no explanation for them. They're just there. And they're not about to go away anytime soon. It's not that easy.

But I don't tell him any of that. He wouldn't understand. He's wealthy and established and confident in going after what he wants, be it a new career, a new woman—a new whatever.

Me, on the other hand, I lack confidence. I'm young and broke and striving to make myself better, but every time I think I've pushed myself into a better place, I fuck it up somehow and end up taking about forty steps backward.

Until I'm right back where I started.

"I don't know," I admit softly. "I'm not sure if this can work out."

"Bryn." His voice breaks on my name and the sound breaks my heart. "Don't do this. Don't say that."

"I was going to give my notice when we returned home," I blurt out, wanting him to know the truth. "I was going to give you two weeks. Then I was going to pack up all my stuff in boxes, shove it into the back of my Saturn, and drive home to Cactus. My grandma said I can stay with her until I get back on my feet and find a job."

Now he looks good and pissed. "You were going to give your notice so you can go back to Cactus? Have you lost your mind?"

I shrug, angry that he would be so insulting. "I have nothing else holding me here." It's a lie. He could hold me here, but I know it wouldn't work out. And it wouldn't be what's best for me. I'd just end up making another mistake and making us both look bad.

He's better off without me. And I don't know if this is true, but I'm probably better off without him too.

"You have nothing else." His voice is monotone, the look in his eyes, blank. "So what happened last night *doesn't* matter."

"Not when it'll end up hurting us, which it will undoubtedly do." I approach him but he takes a step back, like he doesn't want to be near me. "I'm not sure if we're good for each other," I admit.

He stares at me, his mouth set in a grim line. "So you still want to give your notice?"

Slowly, I nod, ignoring the wave of panic that threatens to consume me at my silent confirmation.

"Then I accept your notice. You don't even need to give me two weeks. We're done." His voice, his expression, is final, and I swear I want to burst into great, heaving sobs.

But I don't. I remain quiet, composed. How, I'm not sure.

"I think you should try and call and change your flight

so you can head home tonight," he suggests, his voice clipped. "I'll reimburse you for the change fee which I'm sure will be huge."

"Fine. I'll leave tonight." I lift my chin, refusing to let him see me down. This was what I wanted after all.

Wasn't it?

Chapter Thirteen

Matt

Two weeks later

"YOU ANSWERED." I rub my jaw, the rasp of stubble
prickling across my palm. I haven't shaved in days, and
I've slept like shit.

"You keep calling my damn phone so yeah, I an-
swered," Dad says, sounding downright hostile. "Whatcha want, son?"

I want Bryn. I miss her. I hate what happened between
us, how easily our tentative relationship was destroyed.
Just by a slightly scandalous photo and a few choice
words on a bunch of crappy gossip websites.

Hell, it was a very scandalous photo, leaving Bryn
feeling beyond embarrassed. Vulnerable. I'm used to
those gossipy sites saying a bunch of lies and spreading
rumors. Bryn isn't.

I'd been angry when I left New York. Now I'm just . . . miserable. She left. I'm not exactly sure to where, but I know she couldn't handle being near me another minute longer. Not that I handled our last conversation in New York particularly well. The moment we discovered the article and photo, it all went to hell.

The most amazing night of my life with the most amazing woman I've ever met, ruined. Just like that.

"I want to know why," I finally say, then pause. Waiting for the answer I'm sure will never really come.

"Why what?" Oh, doesn't he sound innocent.

"You know." I take a deep breath, trying to keep my anger under control. "Why did you blab to the media? How much did they pay you? Was it worth it? Having those photos of my innocent assistant spread across the Internet?"

"She didn't look so innocent in that picture." Dad has the nerve to chuckle, the bastard.

I close my eyes, count to five. He's pushing every one of my buttons, and I'm sure the jackass knows it. "I'm used to this sort of treatment. You can drag my name through the mud. I don't care. But you don't bring Bryn into this. She didn't deserve that sort of public humiliation and you know it."

"She humiliated me at your fancy winery party," he says, his voice full of venom. "Believe what you want but you'll see what I did was right for you in the long run. You don't need that silly little tramp dragging you down."

His casual confession makes me sick to my stomach.

I knew he'd done it. Finally hearing him say it reaffirms I'm about to do the right thing. "Bryn James is the best fucking thing that's ever happened to me and you ruined it. Ruined it with your blabbing to the media. I hope they paid you enough to make this all worth it."

"Son, it was completely worth it because it got your name in the public eye again. I bet you've seen an uptick in business with the winery, am I right? You don't want people forgetting you. You're still important you know. A hero to many. Just like I am too," Dad says smugly.

"You're nobody's hero, you fucking asshole. I never want to see or talk to you again." I'm seething. I literally see red, and I pull the phone away from my ear, ready to end the call when I hear his voice.

"Don't cut me off too quick, Matt. I'm the last thing you've got in this world. And you know it."

Not true. I have my friends. Archer and Gage. Ivy and Marina. And if I'm lucky enough, I'll have Bryn back in my life.

"I don't need you," I murmur into the phone, then end the call.

I don't need Vinnie DeLuca at all.

I definitely need my friends though. And more than anything, I need Bryn.

But first, I need to find her.

"IF I THOUGHT you were bad before, you've turned into a complete sullen little girl lately," Archer says with a shake of his head as I stop at the table he's sharing with Gage.

"I don't know if this forty-five-days idea was such a good one after all."

"It wasn't. Fuck the forty-five days." The last thing I'm thinking of is the stupid bet. I settle heavily into a chair, barely looking at the scantily dressed waitress that appears at our table. "Double vodka, straight up. Make it Grey Goose," I mutter.

"Anything else for you guys?" The waitress's voice is bright and cheery. I chance a glance at her, taking in her short skirt, the belly-revealing top that clings to her enormous breasts. I don't bother looking at her face. From the way she's dressed, clearly that's not her intent anyway.

We're at a local sports bar known for its spectacularly gorgeous waitstaff, Archer demanding via text I meet him and Gage there for drinks after work. So here I am, miserable and ready to drown my sorrows in booze.

They're probably somehow trying to tempt me by having us come here. With the bet extension still on, I'm sure they're looking for any way to get me to break it. The waitress is mega hot.

I could give two shits about her. All I want is Bryn.

"We're good right now, thanks," Archer says. His beer bottle is full, as is Gage's. They're both looking at me as if I've lost my mind, I can feel their eyes on me, but I stare at the table, tapping my fingers against the edge of the wood.

"Lack of sex has made you grumpy," Gage starts and I lift my head to glare at him. He shuts up.

"And angry," Archer adds. "What gives?"

Should I tell them? My mood has nothing to do with

lack of sex and everything to do with having the best sex of my life with the most beautiful woman I've ever known. The very same woman who exited my life almost two weeks ago.

The woman I'm in love with but was such a wimp I couldn't even tell her.

"You saw the article on the gossip site right?" I say, figuring I may as well start at the beginning. And come on, have they forgotten already? I know they're wrapped up in their own thing since they're both busy, occupied with work and the women they love.

Lucky bastards.

Plus I've avoided them for fear they'd want to talk about it. Call me out on everything. I've been alone with my misery and finally they forced me to crawl out of my hole.

"Yeah, and the picture. You insisted nothing happened between you two." Archer sends me one of those skeptical, raised eyebrow looks he's so good at. "Not sure if I believe you though. What with Bryn's, uh, panties on display."

"You shouldn't believe me," I say, offering the waitress a grim smile when she sets my drink in front of me, her cleavage practically in my face. Ignoring her boobs, I grab the glass, slam back the vodka with one long swallow and hand it back to her. "Another one, please."

"Right away," she says with a nod before she leaves.

"Damn, dude. Slow down," Gage says. "I don't want to be the one driving your drunk ass home."

I wave a hand. "I'll take a cab."

"No, you won't," Archer says firmly. "Tell us what happened, Matt. Where's Bryn? Ivy says she left. As in left town. Seems sort of extreme."

"She did leave. The article and photo proved too much for her. She quit. Moved back home." I hate my dad for making this happen. Hate even more how he thought he'd been doing me a favor.

I'd been too much for her too, though. She said she'd planned on giving her notice before that stupid article came out. Before we even left for New York. She was going to leave me. After everything that had happened between us, before she would've given me another chance, she would've walked.

Great. I got my chance, and she still bailed. My heart literally fucking hurts at not having her around.

"Where's the waitress with my drink?" I mutter, glaring at Archer and Gage. They both visibly recoil, not that I give a damn. I'm always the nice one. The easygoing guy who doesn't give anyone much shit.

Lately, I am the furthest thing from nice and easygoing. They're all lucky I'm holding it together because I feel like at any moment I could totally lose it.

"Hey." Gage's firm voice makes me meet his gaze. "What happened with you and your dad?"

I shrug. They knew Vinnie was behind this; I told them when I came home. I just haven't talked about it since. I've been too busy wallowing in my misery. "I called and confronted him right after we got back."

"And?"

"And he denied he did it at first. Kept asking why he

would do something like that to his own son, but I kept throwing it back in his face. I never once believed him. I finally broke him down."

I shook my head, offering a whisper of thanks when the waitress returned with a fresh drink. Archer waved her off when she lingered, and I held the glass up to them as if in salute. "He admitted he tipped off the reporter. They spotted Bryn and me at a restaurant in the hotel and took some pictures there. But then they somehow caught sight of us in the hotel room window and decided those were the better photos to put on the site." I drained my glass and set it on the table.

"So your dad is responsible," Gage says, shock in his voice. The look of disgust on my friend's face says it all.

"Yeah. The asshole," I mutter, sadness filling me despite my anger. That my dad could be so heartless and do something like this to me.

It sucks. Our relationship is beyond repair. At least for now. I can't even fathom talking to him again, sharing anything personal with him, even speaking to him casually. Hell, I wouldn't send the man a fucking Christmas card. He's ruined everything.

He'll have to grovel on his hands and knees before I'd consider talking to him again.

"And Bryn left," Gage says.

"She did." I nod, my head a little dizzy. I can feel the alcohol coursing through my blood and I wait for the numbness. I welcome the fucking numbness. "We can call off the bet you know."

"Wait . . . what?" The confused expression on Archer's

face could almost be laughable if I wasn't drowning in my misery.

"Call it off. I won't collect. I can't." I pick up my glass, remember it's empty and set it down again with an irritated growl. "Bryn and I had sex. Amazing, fantastic, never-to-be-had-again sex."

"You sly, lying dog," Gage starts, but Archer shoots him a look. Gage shuts up.

"And she left you anyway. That's tough bro. I'm sorry," Archer says cautiously. Funny how knowing he's about to be a father makes a man suddenly turn compassionate. The Archer of old would've given me endless crap about this.

The new Archer who's madly in love with Ivy and excited about becoming a dad has become . . . considerate of my feelings.

Yes. I'm having a total *Oprah* moment. I blame the vodka.

"Tough doesn't come close to what it is." I smile, but it feels like my face is cracking in two. "Do you know that stupid site ran the article and then they said nothing else? Some other sites picked it up, but then another scandal broke out, I can't even remember what. Rendering me and Bryn long forgotten. That's how much of a nonentity I've become. And you know what? I love that. I don't miss the fans and the photographers and the crap. I miss playing ball. I'll always miss that but otherwise, yeah. I'm over it. I have a new life. A new career that I love and I found a woman I could love too. Instead she leaves me."

Damn, I sound pitiful and morose even to my own ears.

"All right. We're calling off the bet," Archer says, his expression full of worry. "But—"

"You're going to let her go, huh?" Gage asks, interrupting Archer. "Just let her walk away and forget all about her?"

I glare at them both. "What do you mean?" The waitress delivers another shot glass in front of me, much to the disgust of my friends, and I smile gratefully up at her, actually looking in her eyes versus her tits. I wonder if she appreciates that.

Probably not.

"Go after her," Gage urges. "Go to her hometown and tell her you want her back."

I grimace, finish off the contents in my shot glass and then grimace again as the vodka slides down my throat. "You make it sound so easy."

"That's because it is," Gage says with a slight smirk. I'd like to wipe it off his face with my fist. Must be the vodka still talking. "Just hop on a plane and go to that little Podunk town of hers and find her. Can't be that hard to figure out where she lives, her address. When you see her, tell her how you feel."

I let his words sink in and swirl around in my brain along with a heavy dose of vodka. I could do that. Maybe. "What if she rejects me?"

"Then at least you tried," Archer adds. "Then you won't have any regrets or what-ifs. Those what-ifs will kill you, man. Trust me."

Huh. He's right. I wonder how I would even get to Cactus, Texas. Fly into somewhere and rent a car, I assume. I don't know her grandma's name. But I bet everyone would know who Bryn James is. The most beautiful, sweetest, kindest, sexiest woman ever.

"I'll do it." I curl my hand into a fist and pound it on the table, making my shot glasses and the now-empty beer bottles on top of it rattle. "I'll go make flight arrangements right now." I start to stand, but both Archer and Gage wave their arms at me like they're trying to flag my ass down or something.

"Slow your roll, my friend," Gage says, shaking his head with a chuckle as I fall back into my chair, my head spinning. "You need to sober up first. Look at you, three shots of double vodka and you're done for."

"Whatever," I mutter, my mind filled with images of Bryn. Smiling Bryn. Beige Bryn. Naked Bryn. Sad Bryn.

I frown. I never want to see sad Bryn again. I need to find her.

I need to go make that woman mine once and for all.

Chapter Fourteen
_____

Bryn

"GIRL, YOU BETTER clean out that chicken coop and something quick! That rooster looks ready to tear into his girlfriends. He sure don't like walking in shit!"

Sighing, I toss my phone—the very iPhone Matt let me keep despite having purchased it for work purposes— onto my mattress and exit my bedroom to see what my grandma is hollering about now.

She's standing at the kitchen sink washing dishes. I wish we could afford a dishwasher but that's so not happening. Staring out the window, she's watching the chicken coop in the backyard, a fragile-looking structure one of the neighbor boys built for her a few years ago.

"What did you ask me to do?" I sound resigned. Of course, I am, when the only job I can seem to find in this godforsaken town is doing odds and ends for my grandma around the house. I didn't get that job at the

Soap-n-Snip, answering the phone and sweeping up hair. Stacy Jo Nesbitt got that job. She graduated two years after I did, and she already has two babies to take care of.

She deserves the job far more than I do.

"The chicken coop, baby doll. It's a shit storm of epic proportions and that snotty, mean-as-hell rooster hates it when the crap piles up." Grandma cackles again. She loves saying crazy things, shocking people. As she gets older, it gets worse and usually I ignore it or laugh with her.

But today, the very last thing I want to do is laugh. It's hot outside, and I don't want to be out there scooping up chicken crap.

"You want me to clean it out now?" I ask, my shoulders slumping.

"I sure do. Look at that cock." Another cackle. "He's gonna peck the head of every chicken out there if you don't take care of it and quick."

I go to stand next to my grandma and see that she's not exaggerating. The rooster is strutting around in the small fenced-off chicken yard, pecking the head of every poor innocent chicken that approaches him.

Typical male. That rooster is a complete asshole.

"Fine," I say with a sigh. "I'll go clean it."

"Don't forget your waders," she calls to me as I head toward the garage. "And a bucket and a shovel so you can scoop up all that crap!"

I grab the bucket and the shovel she uses special for the chicken coop then slip on the old rubber boots I bought at Walmart years ago that I'd wear when it rained or snowed, which is rare but still. They're white and hideous, scuffed up after years of wear, but I don't care. I'm wearing an old ratty tank top and a pair of denim cut-offs along with them. The people of the great Napa Valley would probably shit themselves if they saw me, but I'm out here in my grandma's backyard with no one around for miles.

I've got nobody to impress.

Rounding the side of the house, I head for the chicken coop and open the gate, thrusting the shovel out to hold back the rooster, who's a mean old jerk that would love nothing more than to jump me from behind and spur me with his claws. He's done it to me before, and I nearly had a heart attack, he scared me so bad.

But this time I'm prepared. You can't turn your back on him or he'll sneak attack you, like your worst enemy.

God, if I really thought about it, I could learn a lot of life lessons out here cleaning up the damn chicken coop. I laugh and shake my head as I start scooping up the chicken poop, which has somehow piled up into little mountains along the inside of their caged area.

It's really freaking disgusting.

It's been a month since I left New York City and went back to St. Helena. I went to the winery early the next morning and cleaned all my personal belongings out of my desk. Gave my notice at my apartment, not caring that I had to pay another month's rent for breaking the lease, even though I was leaving at that very moment.

I just wanted the hell out of there.

It took me a few days to pack up all my stuff, finalize some things, and get everything prepared for the move.

But when I was finally ready to take off, all packed up and headed to the gas station before I went roaring off into the sunset, I decided to check my mail one last time. And found a check from DeLuca Winery—three months' wages. Severance pay, it said on the notes line.

That check both burned my ass and thrilled me down to the bone. I didn't want to take his pity pay, but I also wasn't about to look a gift horse in the mouth, as my grandma would say.

I never did quite get that phrase but whatever. It fit.

So I went to the bank, deposited all that money and then hit the road. It took me six days, but I finally made it only to find myself with no prospects, no energy, and sadder than I've ever been in my life.

I miss Matt. I was dumb, running away from him and my feelings. He'd been so willing to face the troubles beside me head on, and I walked away. Let him go, let him slip right through my fingers like he didn't matter.

God, I'd been such an idiot—I could tear up right now just thinking about it.

But crying over our lost relationship isn't going to bring him back or bring me peace. I messed up, and I needed to face facts. Chalk it up to a mistake made and a lesson learned.

Don't let a good man go, is what my grandma told me when I explained to her what happened a few nights ago. I'd held onto my story, my blow up with Matt for weeks until my grandma finally found me crying on the back porch and point blank asked what the hell was wrong with me.

That had been her one sentence of advice when I finished.

Don't let a good man go.

Too late, Grandma.

Sighing, I rub at my forehead with the heel of my hand before I start scooping up more crap. I should've worn gloves, but I forgot. At least I'm not touching the poop directly, thanks to the shovel.

God, what a transformation I've undergone. One month ago, I was in New York City staying at the most beautiful hotel I've ever seen in my life, and now I'm digging out chicken shit.

Oh, how the mighty have fallen.

I fill up practically the entire bucket with chicken poo, constantly thrusting the shovel in the rooster's direction when he comes at me, always on the defensive around that guy. I'm starting to sweat, I probably stink and my feet feel all squishy and disgusting in the rubber boots.

I'll need a shower as soon as I'm done with this horrendous chore. No wonder my grandma doesn't want to deal with it.

"Bryn?"

I still, turning my head to the left. I swear I just heard Matt's voice call my name. Great. Now I'm going crazy and hearing things.

"Lousy men," I mutter, shaking my head and pointing the shovel at the rooster, who looks ready to jump me at any minute. "You're all alike. Ready to jump on a woman and tear her apart before she can put herself back together again."

"Bryn, what the hell are you doing, talking to a chicken?"

Standing completely straight, I turn slowly, the sun suddenly shining in my eyes. I cover them with my hand to find—

Oh my God, to find Matthew DeLuca standing in my grandma's backyard, on the other side of the chicken coop, looking gorgeous in a pair of khaki shorts and a wine-colored polo shirt.

"I'm not talking to a chicken," I explain, my voice weak. "I'm talking to a rooster."

"Same difference?" Matt asks, a hint of a smile curving his lips.

"Don't tell that to the rooster. You'll only piss him off," I mutter, turning and pointing my shovel at the very creature I'm talking about, who'd gotten closer to me what with my distracted state.

My heart is racing, and I can't believe Matt's standing here. With me.

But why?

"You uh, look good, Bryn."

He's a liar. I look crazy, and I know it. Turning more fully to face him, I kick out one foot, showing off the boots. "You like them?"

"They're interesting. I prefer seeing you in those tiny denim shorts though." He whistles low, a rush of pleasure flowing through me at the sound. "Your legs look mighty long in 'em."

Giddiness courses through me at having him here, with me, in Cactus, Texas, checking out my legs and telling me I look good. If anyone looks good it's him, all sexy and handsome in the shorts and the polo, his dark hair a haphazard mess, his face covered with a shadow of stubble.

If I wasn't dressed like a fool and standing amongst chickens and their crap, I'd run over and throw myself at him.

"Shit!" I yell when a sharp pinch digs into the back of my knees. I turn and swat at the rooster who attacked me. Turn my back on him for a second too long and look at how he treats me. "Goddamn asshole!" I screech, swinging the shovel at him. Thankfully he struts away, and I snatch up the bucket, backing out of the coop until I feel the gate directly behind me. I unlatch it in a hurry and slam it shut, leaning against the chicken wire for a brief, relieved moment as I try and calm my racing heart.

Only to turn around and find Matt laughing at me so hard, I'm afraid he's going to double over and collapse onto the ground.

Matt

I SHOULDN'T LAUGH. Bryn just about got the scare of her life, if the expression on her face was any indication. I hadn't any chance to warn her, and it had been quite shocking to see that rooster fly in the air so fast. One minute we'd been flirting and chatting, the next a wild, puffed-out red rooster came at her, his legs extended and his claws digging right into the back of her legs.

That had been horrifying. The funny part? The curse

words flying out of Bryn's mouth, made even more humorous by her thick accent. She'd been pissed. Furious that the rooster jumped her and tried to take a hunk of her flesh out of her legs.

"That wasn't funny you know," she says as she approaches, which launches me into a fresh round of laughter.

"Oh yes, it was," I say between breaths.

She stops directly in front of me, dropping the bucket by her booted feet. I look at her, really look at her as the laughter dies in my throat. Despite the crazy outfit, she looks hot as hell. The tank top is torn and bleach stained, clinging to her breasts, and those denim shorts should be illegal they're so damn short. I can't help but wonder if she's even wearing any panties underneath because if she is, they're pretty damn tiny.

But those white rubber boots are the finishing touch. I've never seen Bryn look like this.

I kinda like it.

"What are you doing here, Matt?" she asks, sticking the shovel into the ground, her fingers still gripping the handle.

"I came looking for you." My mouth goes dry the longer I stare at her. A faint sheen of sweat covers her skin, and I can smell that addictive-as-hell scent of hers wafting all around me, despite the bucket of chicken shit sitting at her feet.

"Why?" Her voice is so soft, so full of doubt I wish I could pull her in and hold her close.

But I don't. Not yet. I might have to wait until she takes a shower or at the very least washes her hands, but

I will be holding this woman very soon in my arms, I promise.

"I want you to come back with me, Bryn," I tell her, keeping it simple. "I miss you."

Her lips part, and she grips the shovel handle so tight, her knuckles go white. "What?"

"I miss you. Have you missed me too?" I step closer to her, notice the way her eyes widen, her tongue sneaks out for a quick swipe of her lips. Damn, I want to kiss her. "After being without you, I realized I need you."

"As your assistant?"

Ah, my silly Bryn. She just can't believe someone would actually want her, can she? Wouldn't she be surprised, knowing I was a complete wreck while she was gone? "Not as my assistant. I need you in my life. I want you by my side, helping me run the winery."

"Working for you," she says, her voice flat.

"I'll pay you, yes, since technically you'll be my employee but not as my assistant. You'll be my partner." I smile gently and take another step toward her, until I'm standing directly in front of her, reaching out my hand to settle it over hers still gripping the shovel handle. "I'm in love with you, Bryn. And I don't want to live without you anymore."

"Matt," she starts, but I squeeze her hand, silencing her.

"Don't protest or tell me you don't want to bring me down or whatever other crazy excuse you came up with the last time we talked. I don't want to hear it." With my free hand I reach for her, cupping her cheek, savoring her soft,

soft skin. "I want you in my life. I want you living with me in California and working with me. I want us to be partners and grow DeLuca Winery together. What do you think?"

She smiles, her blue eyes bright with tears. "I think you're crazy."

"You're right." Unable to resist any longer, I lean in and press a soft kiss to her tempting lips. "I'm crazy for you, Bryn. Now say that'll you give up scooping chicken shit for the rest of your life and come work with me."

Bryn laughs, the tears flowing freely now. "I don't know. Let me think about it."

"Stubborn woman," I murmur just before I kiss her again, this one deeper, hotter, full of plenty of tongue and sweet, low murmurs of pleasure coming from my woman.

My woman. Mine. That's the only way I've thought of Bryn since she left me. It just took me this long to work up the courage to finally go after the woman I want.

"What about ... what will everyone say?" she asks when she pulls away. "They'll talk about us. About how you're screwing your assistant."

I'm completely offended she would simplify our relationship like that. "I'm not screwing you. I want to be with you. I want you as my partner. In business, in life, in everything. I want you. Fuck anyone who questions that."

She gapes at me like she can't believe what I said. Clearing her throat, she murmurs, "I've been so worried how all of this will affect me. Being with you. I've not had the best luck with men, you know."

"I know," I say softly, my heart breaking for her. She looks scared. Nervous. The very last things I want her to feel. "I would be proud to call you my partner in all aspects of my life, Bryn. You're smart and strong. I need you in my life. More than you can even imagine."

Her eyes shine with unshed tears. "Really?" she asks incredulously.

I dip my head, my mouth hovering above hers. "Really. I love you," I whisper against her lips, as I thrust my fingers into her thick, beautiful hair. "Come home with me, Bryn. Be with me. I need you."

She smiles, a tremulous laugh escaping her before she nods. "I love you too, Matt. I missed you so much. I—I couldn't stand being without you."

"I missed you too, baby. And trust me, I'll never make you scoop up chicken shit at my house. It's one hundred percent chicken shit free." I kiss her again because I can't resist and we both release our grip on the shovel handle at the same time, grabbing hold of each other, our bodies colliding. She feels so damn good next to me, her sexy little body barely covered, looking like my every dream come to life.

Even in the crazy white rubber boots.

"Are you saying you're my own personal savior again? Coming in to rescue me from a life of scooping chicken crap?" She blinks up at me, and I smile, nuzzle my nose against hers.

"Yeah, that's exactly what I'm saying. Only when you call me your savior, I gotta say, you've become mine too." I lower my head and kiss her, wanting her to know how ready I am to take her out of Cactus and bring her home with me for good.

Where she belongs.

Acknowledgments

I HAD A lot of fun writing about these billionaire bachelors and their ridiculous million dollar bet. Creating
the perfect matches for them, watching them fall hard,
I enjoyed every minute of it. I want to thank my editor
Chelsey Emmelhainz for her endless support, for helping me make the books better every single time and her
infinite patience with me while I flailed and generally
worked myself into a complete frenzy throughout the
summer of 2013. I appreciate you more than I think you
know, and I look forward to working on something new
with you!

To everyone at Avon Impulse, I think you're a fabulous
publisher full of amazing support. To Caroline Perny for
being so responsive and for all the help. I've had a great
time being an Avon Impulse author and hope to continue
this journey.

As always, I must thank my family for dealing with

me as I hide away in my office and work all the damn time. I have the best husband and kids EVER.

And to the readers. Your support means the world to me. I wouldn't be able to do this job without you so thank you from the bottom of my heart.

Don't miss how this million-dollar bet got started . . .
Keep reading for excerpts from Book One and Book
Two in Monica Murphy's sexy
Billionaire Bachelors Club series

CRAVE

and

TORN

Now available from Avon Impulse!

An Excerpt from

CRAVE

Ivy

A KNOCK SOUNDS at the door, and I jump, grabbing the robe off the hook with lightning speed. Throwing it on, I approach, figuring it's Gage ready to tell me something lame before he goes to bed. He's always been a little over-protective, so he's probably just checking up on me.

"I'm fine, Gage. Really," I say as I open the door, stunned silent when I see who's standing before me.

"Really?" Archer raises a brow, one hand in his pants' pocket, the other clutching an article of clothing. "Why wouldn't you be anything *but* fine?"

Oh. Shit. He should so not be standing in front of me right now. "What are you doing here?" I whisper, glancing over his shoulder to thankfully see Gage's door is closed.

"Making sure you're comfortable." He thrusts his hand out toward me. "I brought you something."

I'm ultra-aware of the fact that beneath the terry cloth, I'm wearing absolutely nothing. The impulse to untie the sash and let the robe drop to my feet just to see Archer's reaction is near overwhelming.

But I keep it under control. For now.

"What is this?" I take the wadded-up fabric from his hand, our fingers accidentally brushing, and heat rushes through me at first contact.

"One of my T-shirts." He shrugs those broad shoulders, which are still encased in fine white cotton. "I know you didn't have anything to wear to ... bed. Thought I could offer you this."

His eyes darkened at the word *bed* and my knees wobble. Good lord, what this man is doing to me is so completely foreign, I'm not quite sure how to react.

"Um, thanks. I appreciate it." The T-shirt is soft, the fabric thin, as if it's been worn plenty of times, and I have the sudden urge to hold it to my nose and inhale. See if I can somehow smell his scent lingering in the fabric.

The man is clearly turning me into a freak of epic proportions.

"You're welcome." He leans his tall body against the doorframe, looking sleepy and rumpled and way too sexy for words. I want to grab his hand and yank him into my room.

Wait, no I don't. That's a bad—terrible—idea.

Liar.

"Is that all then?" I ask because we don't need to be standing here having this conversation. First, my brother could find us and start in again on what a mistake we are. Second, I'm growing increasingly uncomfortable with the fact that I'm completely naked beneath the robe. Third, I'm still contemplating shedding the robe and showing Archer just how naked I am.

"Yeah. Guess so." His voice is rough, and he pushes away from the doorframe. "Well. Good night."

"Good night," I whisper, but I don't shut the door. I don't move.

Neither does he.

"Ivy . . ." His voice trails off and he clears his throat, looking uncomfortable. Which is hot. Oh my God, everything he does is hot, and I decide to give in to my impulses because screw it.

I want him.

Archer

LIKE AN IDIOT, I can't come up with anything to say. It's like my throat is clogged, and I can hardly force a sound out, what with Ivy standing before me, her long, wavy, dark hair tumbling past her shoulders, her slender body engulfed in the thick white robe I keep for guests. The very same type of robe we provide at Hush.

But then she does something so surprising—so amazingly awesome—I'm momentarily dumbfounded by the sight.

Her slender hands go for the belt of the robe and she

undoes it quickly, the fabric parting, revealing bare skin. Completely bare skin.

Holy shit. She's naked. And she just dumped the robe onto the ground so she's standing in front of me. Again, I must stress, naked.

My mouth drops open, a rough sound coming from low in my throat. Damn, she's gorgeous. All long legs and curvy waist and hips and full breasts topped with pretty pink nipples. I'm completely entranced for a long, agonizing moment. All I can do is gape at her.

"Well, are you just going to stand there and wait for my brother to come back out and find us like this or are you going to come inside my room?"

Marina

"THIS IS A huge mistake."

"What is?" He settles those big hands of his on my waist. His long fingers span outward, gripping me tight, and I feel like I've become seized by some uncontrollable force, one I can't fight off no matter how hard I try.

That force would be Gage.

"I already told you." God, he's exasperating. It's like he doesn't even listen to a word I say. "Us. Together. There will never be an *us* or a *together*, got it?"

"Got it, boss." He's not really listening, I can tell. He's pulled slightly away so he can stare down at me, too enraptured with his hands on my body. A shock of brown hair tinged with gold tumbles down across his forehead, and I resist the urge to reach out and push it away from his face.

Just barely.

He slides his hands around me until they settle at the small of my back, his fingertips barely grazing my backside. I'm wearing jeans, yet it's like I can feel his touch directly on my skin. Heat rushes over me, making my head spin, and I let go of a shaky exhalation.

"We shouldn't do this," I whisper, pressing my lips together when I feel his hands slide over my butt. Oh my God, his touch feels so good.

What the hell am I *thinking*? Letting him touch me like this? It's wrong. Us together is wrong.

So why does it feel so right?

"Do what?" His question sounds innocent enough, but his touch isn't. He pulls me into him so I can feel the unmistakable ridge of his erection pressing against my belly and a gasp escapes me. He's big. Thick. My thighs shake at the thought of him entering me.

I need to put a stop to this, and quick.

"I don't think we sh—"

Gage presses his index finger to my lips, silencing me. I stare up at him, entranced by the glow in his eyes, the way he stares at my mouth. Like he's a starving man dying to devour me.

Anticipation thrums through my veins. I should walk away now. Right now, before we take this any further. We're standing in the doorway of the bakery for God's sake. Anyone could see us, not that many people are roaming the downtown sidewalks at this time of night. He's got one hand sprawled across my ass and he's tracing my lips with his finger like he wants to memorize the shape of them.

And I'm ... parting my lips so I can suck on his fingertip.

His eyes darken as he slips his finger deeper into my mouth. I close my lips around him, sucking, tasting his salty skin with a flick of my tongue. A rough, masculine sound rumbles from his chest as his hand falls away from my lips. He drifts his fingers down my chin, my neck, and my breath catches in my throat.

"Gage." I whisper his name, confused. Is it a plea for him to stop or for him to continue? I don't know. I don't know what I want from him.

"Scared?" he asks, his lids lifting so he can pin me with his gorgeous green eyes. They're glittering in the semidarkness, full of so much hunger, and my body responds, pulsating with need.

I try my best to offer a snide response but the truth comes out instead. "Terrified."

He lowers his head. I can feel his breath feather across my lips, and I part them in response, eager for his kiss. "That makes two of us," he whispers.

Just before he settles his mouth on mine.

About the Author

New York Times and *USA Today* bestselling author MONICA MURPHY is a native Californian who lives in the foothills below Yosemite. A wife and mother of three, she writes new adult and contemporary romance. Visit her online at www.monicamurphyauthor.com and on Facebook at www.facebook.com/MonicaMurphyAuthor.

Visit www.AuthorTracker.com for exclusive information on your favorite HarperCollins authors.

Give in to your impulses . . .
Read on for a sneak peek at four brand-new
e-book original tales of romance
from Avon Books.
Available now wherever e-books are sold.

ALL I WANT FOR CHRISTMAS IS A COWBOY
By Emma Cane, Jennifer Ryan, and Katie Lane

SANTA, BRING MY BABY BACK
By Cheryl Harper

THE CHRISTMAS COOKIE CHRONICLES: GRACE
By Lori Wilde

DESPERATELY SEEKING FIREMAN
A BACHELOR FIREMEN NOVELLA
By Jennifer Bernard

ALL I WANT FOR CHRISTMAS IS A COWBOY

by *Emma Cane, Jennifer Ryan, and Katie Lane*

What's better than Christmas?
Christmas and Cowboys.

From Emma Cane, Jennifer Ryan, and Katie Lane come three wildly romantic holiday stories featuring snowstorms, proposals, a sleigh ride . . . and, yes, cowboys.

The Christmas Cabin by Emma Cane

Sandy and her five-year-old son, Nate, are Christmas tree–hunting when a snowstorm strikes and an old ranch hand points them to an abandoned cabin. Little does Sandy know, the hand sent cowboy Doug Thalberg to the same place. It's a Christmas all of Valentine Valley will remember.

Can't Wait by Jennifer Ryan

Before The Hunted Series began . . .

Though she is the woman of his dreams, Caleb Bowden knows his best friend's sister, Summer Turner, is off limits. He won't cross that line, which means Summer will just have to take matters into her own hands if she wants her cowboy for Christmas.

Baby It's Cold Outside by Katie Lane

Alana Hale hits the internet dating jackpot when she finds Clint McCormick. He's sensitive and responsible—not to mention wealthy. When he invites her to spend the holidays on his family's ranch, she readily accepts. But on the way there, a blizzard strands her with a womanizing rodeo cowboy who could change everything . . .

An Excerpt from

SANTA, BRING MY BABY BACK

by Cheryl Harper

A bride abandoned at the altar . . . just in time for Christmas? 'Tis the season for second chances at Cheryl Harper's Elvis-themed Rock'n'Rolla Hotel.

There was something about Grace Andersen that made him want to help, even after decades of trying to guard his mother and her money against personalities and stories like hers.

He wouldn't mind being Grace Andersen's hero.

To avoid doing something stupid, Charlie turned to go but stopped when she added, "Oh, Charlie, could you do me a favor?"

She shuffled toward him, the rustle of the wedding dress sweeping the floor loud in the silence. "Could you unzip me? I thought I was going to dislocate a shoulder getting it zipped in the first place." She turned and bent her head so that all Charlie could see was the smooth, pale skin of her shoulders and the loose dark hairs that tickled her neck.

When he didn't move quickly enough, she turned her head to look at him over one perfect shoulder.

Remembering to breathe became a struggle again.

He forced himself to step closer. He grasped the zipper with one hand and slid the other under the fabric. The zipper made a quiet hiss as it slid down the curve of her back, every centimeter showing more beautiful skin.

And out of the blue he wondered if unzipping Grace Andersen would ever get old. Finished, he took two steps away to keep from smoothing his hands over her shoulders like he wanted, or tracing a finger down her spine just to see goose bumps.

She turned her head. "Thanks."

As he pulled the door closed behind him, Charlie tried to remember the last time he'd seen anyone as pretty as she was in real life. Never. But she wasn't his type. He preferred career women who wore glasses and looked like they could reel off stock prices or legal precedents. He liked women with sharp minds and sturdy savings. He'd had enough excitement growing up with Willodean McMinn Holloway Luttrell Jackson. Now all he wanted was a comfortable home, an easy, companionable, stable relationship, and maybe a baby to keep things interesting. Maybe.

Grace Andersen looked like . . . magic.

He propped his hands on his hips and shook his head as he looked out at the guitar-shaped pool that was covered for the season.

Magic? He hadn't been in the hotel for a full twenty-four hours and already his mind was going. Something about being that close to her had melted it. But Grace Andersen was just a woman. She'd been left at the altar but didn't seem too broken up about it. He hoped her new plan, whatever it was, included checking out of the hotel immediately. Beautiful Grace Andersen might have the ability to wreck his goals along with his logic if she stayed.

An Excerpt from

THE CHRISTMAS COOKIE CHRONICLES: GRACE

by Lori Wilde

(Originally appeared in the print anthology
The Christmas Cookie Collection)

New York Times bestselling author
Lori Wilde returns to Twilight, Texas, for
another delightful holiday installment of
her *Christmas Cookie Chronicles*. And this
time, a young couple are thrilled to expect
the greatest gift of all: a new baby!

The perfect Christmas starts with the perfect tree . . .

Flynn MacGregor Calloway put a palm to her aching back, wrapped her other arm around her pregnant belly, canted her head, and studied the spindly-branched, lopsided Scotch pine. After much wrestling and a few choice words, she'd managed to get it set up in a corner of the living room in the cottage she shared with her husband, Jesse.

She'd wanted to surprise him, so she'd waited until after the morning wedding of Jesse's father, Sheriff Hondo Crouch, and his bride, Patsy Cross, before she'd slipped down to the Christmas tree lot and, using Jesse's pickup truck, drove the tree home. Jesse had volunteered to drive the newlyweds to DFW airport to catch a plane bound for a Hawaii honeymoon, so he had taken their sedan because three people and luggage fit in it better, giving Flynn plenty of time to get it done.

The glow from the icicle lights dangling on the eaves outside slanted through the window and shone through some of the more meager limbs.

Okay, so it wasn't quite a Charlie Brown tree, but it was close and clearly not what Maven Styles, the author of *How to Host the Perfect Christmas*, had in mind when she declared that an impeccable holiday began with the perfect tree.

Then again, Maven Styles probably wasn't on a newlywed student's tight budget that required her to wait for Christmas Eve, when they marked down the trees. Flynn had picked this one up for five dollars, and she was proud of her bargain. Maybe not proud, but it was a real tree, not artificial, and seven feet tall. She should get points for that, right? All it needed were a few decorations to spiff it up.

She couldn't regret cutting corners. The baby had been a surprise, a very welcome surprise to be sure, but their finances had taken an added hit because of it. Between scraping together money for her college tuition, the cost of rebuilding Jesse's motorcycle shop after the fire, exorbitant health insurance for the self-employed, and getting ready for the baby's arrival, they hadn't much money left to spend on holiday celebrations. Their situation was a temporary setback, she knew that, but part of her couldn't help feeling wistful that their last Christmas with just the two of them was going to be as sparse as that scraggly Scotch pine.

Stop feeling sorry for yourself, she scolded. *Plenty of people have it much worse.*

By tightly pinching pennies all year and keeping an eagle eye out for sales, she'd managed to save just enough to buy Jesse a new leather jacket to replace the one he'd worn since high school. She couldn't wait to give it to him on Christmas morning. For now, it was wrapped and stowed in the trunk of their car. He'd had so little growing up that she ached to give him everything his heart desired. Which was why she'd checked *How to Host the Perfect Christmas* out of the library, hoping she could pick up a few pointers.

A cardboard box filled with decorations from her childhood sat on the floor. Flynn peeled back the tape and opened the flaps. Her mother had had the habit of either buying or making one special ornament to commemorate each Christmas.

As she removed them from the box, each decoration stirred a memory—the candy canes made out of bread dough and shellacked (crumbling a bit now with age) that she and her younger sister, Carrie, had helped their mother bake in 1992. The twin wooden toy soldiers her mother's best friend, Marva Bullock, had given her after the twins, Noah and Joel, were born; and the last ornament her mother had ever purchased, a delicate red glass ball inset with a tiny nativity scene.

Air stilled in her lungs. Although her family hadn't known it at the time, the red glass ball represented the last perfect Christmas before her mother had been diagnosed with amyotrophic lateral sclerosis.

Tears misted her eyes. *Oh, Mama. You'll never know your grandchildren.* With a knuckle, she wiped away the tears. Should she put the ornament on the tree? It would stir painful memories every time she looked at it. And yet the ornament was a shining reminder of that one perfect Christmas when her family was last together and whole.

An Excerpt from

DESPERATELY SEEKING FIREMAN
A Bachelor Firemen Novella
by Jennifer Bernard

From *USA Today* bestseller Jennifer Bernard
comes the steamy story of a sexy bachelor fireman
and the woman who will turn his life around.

The groom's side of the aisle was packed with an astonishingly high number of gorgeous men. Nita Moreno, standing near Melissa McGuire—soon to be Melissa Brody—surveyed the pews with widening eyes. There was enough testosterone in the building to fuel a small nation's army. Enough handsome, manly faces to fill an issue of *Playgirl*. Enough brawny muscles to . . .

Oops. Busted. From across the aisle, two steps behind Captain Brody, a pair of amused, tiger-striped eyes met hers. An unusual mixture of gold and green, surrounded by thick black eyelashes, they would have made their owner look feminine if he weren't one solid hunk of hard-packed male. A smile twitched at the corner of his mouth. Even in this context—the so-called Bachelor Firemen crowding the wedding of their revered fire captain—he stood out. First there was that breath-taking physique. Then there was his face, a study in contrasts. His features were so strong they almost qualified as harsh. Firm jaw, uncompromising cheekbones. A man's man . . . until one looked into those golden eyes, or noticed that he possessed the most beautiful mouth Nita had ever seen on a man.

She narrowed her own eyes and met him look for look. Hey, she wasn't checking out the available men. She had one of her own. Very deliberately, she let her gaze roam to the bride's side of the aisle and settle on Bradford Maddox the Fourth. Hedge fund operator, family scion, possessor of a killer business instinct and an only-slightly-receding hairline, he was hers, and she could still scarcely believe it. Maybe soon she and Bradford would be making their way down an aisle like this. Out of unconscious habit, she took the inside of her cheek between her teeth and worried it at. She loved Bradford, and she knew he felt the same. He must.

Bradford, who seemed lost in thought, startled when he realized she was looking adoringly at him. He gave her a faint smile, then pressed his finger to his ear. Lovely. He wasn't lost in thought, he was listening to his Bluetooth. She sighed, telling herself to let it go. It came with the territory when you dated a hotshot financier. Of course he couldn't focus his *entire* attention on the wedding of two people he didn't even know.

The right side of her body felt suddenly warm, and she realized the man across the aisle was still watching her, as if she fascinated him.

Really? *She* fascinated *him?* That seemed unlikely. She

raised a questioning eyebrow at him. He smiled, the expression transforming his face from the inside out. Goodness, the man was gorgeous, in a totally different way from Bradford. Dark instead of blond, tough instead of charming. Virile and primitive, the kind of man who would toss you over his shoulder and have his way with you.

He jerked his chin at her, as if signaling her to meet him in the chancel.

She frowned at him, scolding. *Excuse me?* How inappropriate.

He did it again, more urgently this time.

What did the man want? She lifted her hands, palms up—a frustrated question—as he mouthed something to her.

"Bouquet."

Aw, crap.